I0548343

*Magical Invasion*

The Signaler was now trembling, her mouth open in amazement as she also stared into the sky.

"What is it?" Handrick demanded. "Grand Liaison, what do you see?"

A string of drool emerged from one corner of his mouth as the man spoke around his food. "It is a great bird; a phoenix of power clothed in red, blue and purple. It has taken flight from the great city and adorned its brightest plumage to attract us; to lure us as its mate to pursue it for the glory of the Signaler's Guild."

"What did he say?" demanded an exasperated Intona.

"The Signalers in the city have just communicated that they have the gates," Handrick said, studying the Grand Liaison for some sign that what he was saying was accurate. "Correct, Grand Liaison?"

"The magnificent general has spoken the truth and indeed it is so. The glorious sisters on their mission of stealth have brought forth the lamp of education to shine upon our ignorance," he half-sang.

"Get everyone on their feet," growled Handrick, cutting the fat man off before he burst completely into song. "Bring everyone up even with the tree line; weapons in their hands and ready to move."

Handrick smelled a host of odors on the breeze; the stench of over-ripe pomegranate from the perfume on the Grand Liaison, the combined smell of fear and anticipation from the human soldiers, and the faint scent of a sleeping mok curled somewhere nearby in its deep burrow. Once he received the signal that the soldiers were in place all would be ready; the invasion would finally begin in earnest. His horse hopped eagerly from hoof to hoof, picking up the excitement of its rider as the Were watched for the waving of the flag that would come from his left. The anticipation was enormous and Handrick almost remembered what it was like to be young again.

Then it came, a single flash of white within the stygian darkness of the trees. No human could have seen it; but he had.

# Jamus' Sorrow

by Trevis Powell

A BlackWyrm Book
Louisville, Kentucky

JAMUS' SORROW

Copyright ©2011 by BlackWyrm

A BlackWyrm Book
BlackWyrm Publishing
10307 Chimney Ridge Ct, Louisville, KY 40299

Printed in the United States of America.

ISBN: 978-1-61318-118-8
LCCN: 2011932475

Cover design by Dave Mattingly
Edited by Stella Davis

First edition: July 2011

To Alisha, Heather, Matt and Lauren; God's gifts to me.

# Prologue

"Gran, it's a Were," Tomo cried, dropping the arrow he held and working desperately to open a long pouch in the back of his quiver. Jamus threw aside his bow completely and with a trembling hand drew a dagger from his belt; the edge of the blade shining oddly in the moonlight. Mute continued to run towards them; the wolf some distance behind but closing rapidly; it was unclear whether he would reach the camp before the beast caught him. Gran burst from the tent in a shower of snow, her silver coated frying pan gripped tightly in both hands.

Fear flooded them all and Gran's grin looked like that of a skull as she lifted her makeshift weapon and Tomo pulled forth the three silver-tipped arrows Jamus had provided for him. In step they moved towards Mute in a grim line; knowing that their weapons were capable of damaging the Were but also aware that some of them would likely die in this fight.

"Here doggy, doggy," Gran whispered under her breath, her eyes shining with tears.

Tomo almost felt a flash of confidence at the old woman's anticipation, but it died immediately in the next instant.

That's when the second Were growled behind them.

# Chapter One

Clawing at the cold ground the slave worked to find purchase with his torn and bleeding fingers as he struggled to drag the immeasurable weight through the thick forest. His mind was as numb as his bare toes but his back enjoyed no such blessing as the pain of raw wounds inflicted by the taskmaster's whip competed with that of muscles torn by the unending strain. How long had the slave suffered under this demon? How many weeks, months, or had it been years? Why would not death come to release him?

The same trees that impeded his progress also offered him the only purchase he could find. A tree trunk or the up-thrust curve of a root occasionally came within his reach and allowed him to move forward one more step; dragging the weight forward just a little further to the place where he would collapse and die only to be replaced by another so the endless march could go on. But death no longer held any fear for the slave; he longed for that moment of blessed release from the unendurable agonies of this world.

"Faster," roared the demon, or rather demoness, from her seat upon his burden.

She punctuated her order with yet another snap of the whip; a magical creation that could be as long or as short as needed to reach the slave wherever the demoness might be. Multiple ends held jagged tips cursed with pain-inducing poison meant to strip away the last bit of his willpower and leave him a mindless husk that would pull until his heart exploded in his chest. How much longer could that be? How much longer could he endure such torture? Why not just give up now?

The burden itself was a wicked construction; designed to resist all attempts at moving it even if the ground had been flat and unobstructed. It was made of some type of devilish wood that weighed as heavily as stone and sunk deep into the forest loam so that the slave was plowing a furrow with each small step he managed. It was a killing weight even without she who rode upon it. The slave himself had been forced to build it under the supervision of this same devil. Even worse; atop it sat not only the demoness but another who weighed even more than did she.

In every conceivable way the demonic overseer had cunningly designed his task to be both impossible and torturous; allowing the slave only an occasional mouthful of food and even less water. For clothing the slave had only the remnants of what in better times had been a silken robe that now hung in tatters doing nothing for his modesty and less to protect him from the deepening cold; and even that had been soaked in dried blood until it became stiff and uncomfortable.

Only his hate kept him going now; hatred of the demoness and hatred for the one who had killed his wife and left him to this terrible fate. Hate was all that remained to him and so he dug in his toes once more, easing the burden forward once again as the cruel chains dug into his shoulders and caused his weeping sores to blossom again. Hate was all that he lived for but the end of his endurance was near.

Collapsing for the hundredth time this day the slave lay with his frost-bitten face against the cold, cold ground and gasped for air. His lungs were near bursting from his exertions but the demoness cared not; the slave could hear her lifting her cursed whip for another strike; perhaps the one that would finally kill him.

"Get up, you weakling," she roared; her voice like the grating of stone on stone. "We cannot stop yet; we have to keep moving."

The slave tried to move but couldn't find the strength; his fingers clenched weakly at the frozen mud while one foot scrabbled ineffectively. He knew he was finished. He could go no further.

"Get up."

"I cannot," wailed the slave.

"Get up, I'm warning you!"

"I cannot, let me die here."

"You'll get up or rue the day!" the demoness threatened, then added, "like as not."

Crack! The sting of the whip across his backside had the slave up and moving at record speed; the demoness cackling in glee at the forward progress. Unfortunately the burst of energy was short lived, and the slave collapsed again after moving no more than twice his own body length.

"I'm dying," the slave moaned.

The demoness considered using her switch again but decided the man needed a break. She looked back in the direction they had come and realized that she could still see the camp they had left more than an hour ago.

"You're soft, boy," she wheezed, laying back in exhaustion on the litter. Reaching out one trembling hand she tenderly touched her companion's brow. Confident that he still showed no signs of fever, she lay back to gather her strength; they couldn't afford to rest for long and the nobleman dragging their makeshift litter was not strong enough to drag them both indefinitely.

Gran lay looking up into the nearly bare branches towards the darkening sky. Clouds were moving in and the wind held the bite of snow on it; if it didn't fall today it surely would tonight. She wasn't sure any of them could survive another bitter night. Lord Gelbow was all but nude; having fled the overturned carriage wearing nothing but a silk dressing gown and a pair of woolen socks. Gran had surrendered her cloak and walking staff, and then commandeered most of the man's robe to build the travois she reclined upon, but thankfully they had quilts to keep off some of the chill. The fellow on the sled beside her was likely dying no matter what.

"You're going to be fine, son, like as not," she argued aloud with herself, patting the hand of the unmoving man. He didn't respond; he hadn't regained consciousness since the fight the day before.

Her head was spinning so the elderly woman closed her eyes for a moment; trying to clear it by concentrating on the sounds and smells around her as she had been taught as a youth. The sounds were easy to identify; the heavy breathing of Viscount Gelbow overtopped all with that of the wounded man beside her barely registering. Birds were calling but not many; most had already fled for warmer climes. It was much too late in the season for insects and the noise of their passage had frightened most small animals into hiding. As for smells she couldn't detect anything over the untanned hides the wounded man wore and the unwashed bodies of the three of them. Somehow Lord Gelbow still carried a faint hint of lilac perfume.

"When everyone stinks, trust a dandy to still smell the best," she quoted, recalling the old story about the Jackdog and the Paunchy Prince. She didn't realize that she had spoken aloud until the viscount spoke.

"I beg your pardon?" he puffed, unsure of what she was talking about but reasonably sure it was meant as an insult towards him.

"I said you're soft, boy," she wheezed. "You can't even drag the two of us from one tree to the next without passing out."

Easing himself to his knees the viscount gave a piteous look at Gran. "I'm a landed noble, Gran, not a plow horse."

"You're soft and lazy," Gran announced, her head sagging weakly back to her makeshift pillow. She wasn't in much better shape than the woodsman.

Crawling back to them Jamus Gelbow peeled back the dressing around the woodsman's chest and peeked beneath it; the skin remained raw but he smelled no sign of pestilence.

"You're certain the arrow didn't penetrate?" he asked, prudently moving out of the reach of Gran's switch.

Too tired to even challenge the noble's questioning of her word Gran only replied. "The arrow struck the rib and broke it; the bone took most of the force but he lost a lot of blood when we were unconscious after the wreck. That's the danger now."

Jamus looked askance at the old woman, more worried for her than the woodsman. How she was even awake was beyond him. Her leg was broken; he was certain about that, and the blow she had taken when her head struck a stone on the road had looked fatal. It looked at least as bad as had, the noble swallowed back a sob of despair, the wound that had killed his wife.

"Why should blood loss be such an issue? Isn't that how healers let poisons out of the body?"

Gran summoned up the strength to open one eye to glare weakly at the man.

"I don't have time for foolishness or the stupidity of backstreet charlatans," she stated weakly, her voice trailing away. She might be dying but she still had fire. "Now get us moving again!"

Jamus reluctantly climbed to his feet and took up the ropes Gran had made by cutting strips of leather from the unconscious woodsman's shirt and began dragging the travois along the path. He whimpered occasionally at the pain but he kept on, looking back often to see if his passengers were still breathing.

He had been the first to awaken after the carriage had flipped over. His wife's head had been cradled in his lap when it happened and her stiffening body was lying atop him when he came to. She was dead, no question, and had been so even before the crash. Jamus allowed another moment of grief to overcome him; how would he ever live without Eldena?

Gran had been lying atop them both and she hadn't been moving either; at first Jamus thought that she was also dead. The woodsman was nearby when Jamus crawled free of the wreckage but there was no sign of Conn, his driver, or the youth that had dragged Gran into the carriage. Conn was dead, Jamus knew, but in the shock of seeing his wife die couldn't remember where the man's body had fallen.

Shaken but mostly uninjured Jamus had come to hearing the growling of animals, and figured that wolves or bears were fighting over the bodies of the dead horses still attached to the carriage. A Quarg war horn had urged him to believe it was the former, Gran had told him how the humanoids trained the wolves, and had expected at any moment for one of the barbarians to find him.

Pulling Gran from the carriage had been easy; the whole roof had fallen off when the carriage overturned, and the woodsman was already free of the wreckage. After wrapping them in quilts that had fallen from the carriage, he had dragged them both a short distance into the woods and concealed them in a thicket. Next Jamus had returned for the body of his wife, and laid her to rest in the forest. It was her people's way for their remains to be left for the animals to consume but it had been hard to leave her like that. Returning one last time to the carriage he had thought to get some clothes for himself, or at the least pry off some of the semi-precious stones the carriage had been decorated with to buy some, but one look at the beast sniffing around the carriage had convinced him that it was time to leave. The wind blew from the beast, filling Jamus' nose with the stink of unwashed animal and clotting blood and he knew it immediately for a Were.

It had been a Were that stopped their carriage initially and Jamus had no way of knowing if this was the same one or not, and really didn't care either way. It was a killer beast and would tear him to shreds on sight. The creature was in his half-man, half-wolf form and seemed to be searching about the wreckage, probably for something, or someone, to consume. From the corners of its mouth dripped white foam that told Jamus that even beyond the Curse it carried, the beast was diseased as well. Moving quietly back into the underbrush Jamus wondered what had happened to his foil; the weapon was of little use in most fights but it had a magical point that might have frightened the Were away. It was then that he had found the odd-looking steel contraption. Made of thin bars and leather straps; it had what looked to be a spoon mounted on one side with a spring attached. Unsure exactly what it was Jamus had taken it for a weapon; it might work as a club.

And what of the Quargs? He had heard the horns; there should have been dozens of the humanoids, hundreds perhaps, swarming over the carriage as soon as it toppled. Weres and wolves didn't shoot arrows, after all. Frightened but knowing it was necessary, Jamus had moved as quietly as he was able to a point where he could view the road beyond the carriage, and had been amazed at the numbers of bodies laying there.

Quargs, yes, and wolves as well. Dozens lay strewn about in various pieces; few if any were whole. Some had been partially eaten and others torn limb from limb; there were no wounded in view; apparently the Were had finished them all.

Jamus then returned to Gran and the woodsman, expecting them both to be dead. There were not, surprisingly, so he had done what he could for their wounds. One last time he had returned to his wife's body and there removed a few coins she had sewn into her clothing; she was always the smart one. Giving her frigid lips one last kiss Jamus had returned to his patients and lay between them; trying to cry himself to sleep as he warmed them but even through his despair fear had kept him awake; there were too many enemies about. The wolves had howled all night long.

This morning Gran had awakened him and demanded that he build the travois. Could that really be less than an hour ago? Jamus removed his ragged robe and retied it as a makeshift loincloth, then trudged on.

Progress remained sluggish as Jamus continued his slow march. Occasionally Quarg horns blew to the north so they were traveling south; it seemed as good a direction as any and the trail pointed that way. Twice someone or something big had stumbled through a thicket in the forest nearby, prompting them to hide. There had not been time to pull the travois from the trail; and no where to conceal it if Jamus had, so all he could do was crouch down where they were and pray that no one else was following the same trail. By noon Gran was asleep and the noble's nerves were on edge; it was nothing short of a miracle that they had not yet been found.

Jamus' spirits rose slightly when he first heard and then saw a tiny stream of water running down a hillside and crossing his path. The stream's bed was covered in stones thick with green moss, indicating that the water didn't run all the time, but the nobleman couldn't have cared less as he stuck his face into a pool. The water was bitterly cold but gloriously wet and Jamus lapped up as much as he could hold. Once his thirst was slaked he cupped some in his hands to carry to the others but barely arrived with enough to wet Gran's lips.

Looking for a better way Jamus looked through their meager possessions for something to both bring the wounded a drink and carry some with them for later. The big woodsman had a pack but no water skin; although Jamus was happy to find some dried meat there. Gran's cloak, now the bottom of the travois, held several large pockets but nothing that would carry water; a thimble being the best option.

Almost Jamus returned to scooping the water with his hands; perhaps they might get enough to survive if barely, when an inspiration struck him. Moving to the stranger's feet Jamus pulled the man's leather shoes free and, after washing them as best he could in the stream, filled one with water and brought it to Gran. Without truly waking the old woman drained the semi-waterproof shoe twice. Her companion didn't do so well, though he did swallow by reflex when the water was poured into his mouth. Filling both shoes Jamus placed them carefully on the travois, braced them from tipping over by his metal 'club', and drank from the stream again; he hoped not to have to drink from the boots himself.

Muscles screaming in protest Jamus moved on down the trail. Water sources were not were you wanted to rest at if you needed to hide; he'd read that in a book somewhere, or heard it in a tavern; it was hard to remember which as he had likely been drinking on both occasions. Sooner or later everyone would come to water; including your enemies.

Exhaustion seemed imminent as the nobleman pulled the travois along. He alternated pulling the knotted ropes with lifting the ends of the two branches of the base and dragging it along in that manner to give one group of muscles a rest while ruining the others but he couldn't keep up the pace for long. Sinking to his knees Jamus gasped for air as his legs trembled from the strain as he watched the first snowflakes fall; he'd have to find shelter soon.

A gambling man, Jamus would have given long odds that he would be unable to travel anymore on this day; must less pull the travois along as well. But then a howl arose from a shockingly close distance; somewhere back down the trail. In a burst of desperation he snatched up the poles and began to run ,not really believing that he had a chance to escape. That had been the howl of a Were.

# Chapter Two

For three days they had entered Aldrigal City in ones and twos; taking up sleeping space in the common rooms of inns throughout the city. Half were in the Merchant's Quarter and they came the closest to arousing suspicion. Over the years that quarter had become the place where the richest citizens of the city built their lavish homes and the area was encircled by the stoutest walls and protected by private guardsmen. Were any of those who lived there hiring new mercenaries? The rumors spread wildly that something was up; but the orders came long before anything could come of it.

Those who stayed elsewhere in the city were not entirely unnoticed. Some were young, and had never seen a city the size of the Aldrigal capitol. They had a difficult time not falling prey to the myriad pitfalls a young man with a little coin in his purse can find in such a place; and the older men assigned to them had their hands full keeping their wards out of trouble. In the end, though a handful of their number wound up in the Aldrigal public prison, a deep pit in the Old Quarter accessible only when a rope was lowered down into it, the bulk of the Firthian troops were available and sober when the call came.

It was after midnight when they assembled; the night was dark and the air more than chill. Remnants of a recent fall festival still clung to the trees of the park where the First Firthian Light Foot came together; colorful streamers blew in the breeze and the corpse of a man the city watch had not as of yet discovered lay draped over a thick branch half-way up a tall sycamore. They had the easy task; taking the main city gates and dispersing the city watch, then holding the gates until relief arrived. It was the Second Firthian Light Foot who faced the task of defeating the private mercenaries in the Merchant's Quarter. If their relief never came, at least those holding the gates might have an opportunity to flee the city. The Second would be trapped.

Keeping as quiet as armed men can be in the dark, the First Foot waited as their officers counted them.

"Only three missing," reported the Calque, or sub-captain to his Captain. "That's better than we hoped."

"Two are in jail," added the sergeant. "I don't know what happened to Greener."

"Probably knifed in some alley," commented the captain. "Nothing we can do about him now; if he was taken and talked, we'll all soon be dead regardless."

Murmuring their agreement the others went without further comment; they were all nervous and such talk didn't help steady them any. They had served together long enough to share such misgivings among themselves but were careful to say nothing within earshot of their men.

"Everyone had their weapons?" the captain asked, attempting to alleviate some of the tension with the standard military joke about young soldiers showing up for a battle having forgotten to bring their both their weapons and their trousers.

It was the sergeant, always ready with a quip, who responded. "Aye sir, but half will be going into battle with their backsides shining in the moonlight."

They chuckled a trifle louder than was necessary so that their mirth and apparent lack of nervousness would drift to the waiting men.

"Alright then, gentlemen, as we planned; Calque you will lead two squads to assault the City Watch's barracks; don't waste any time once you get in sight of the building; storm it and take it before they can wake and arm themselves. Kill all you must and drop the others into the pit. Arm any prisoners that you free and set them loose to pillage if you think they're up for it, then dispatch one squad to aid me and lead the other to ensure Second took the Merchant Quarter gate. Clean the streets as you go; I don't want any of the city watch choosing a rally point anywhere along the streets between the Merchant Quarter and the main gates. Sergeant you will take your squad to the main square in the Old Quarter and act as reserve; do not hesitate to kill anyone you see carrying a weapon and respond wherever you think you are needed. I will lead the last squad in an assault on the main gate. Do we have our Signaler?"

"She's here, Sir," drawled the sergeant. "And is giving the men the creeps as always."

"They'll be glad for her if she's needed," the captain stated. No one was happy with the presence of the woman; but she had abilities they did not and, after all, orders were orders.

"I'm just happy that she'll be with you, Captain," the sergeant said, smiling. He was older than the other men by almost two decades and had trained them both; he was allowed a certain amount of cheekiness. "With her around it would be difficult fighting with the skin trying to crawl off my back."

Smiling the captain worked a sizeable quantity of chaw into his cheek and spit once to get the juices properly flowing before he spoke again. "That's why I intend to lead from behind this time; so I can keep an eye on her."

"She's not that good looking," stated the sergeant, comically rolling his eyes.

"She's not at all good looking," rejoined the captain.

"The men are getting restless," commented the calque, whose nervousness was beginning to show. "Is it time yet?"

Both officers looked at the sergeant, who in turn took a step back and looked up at the stars. Pausing only a moment he replied, "Yes sir, it looks about right."

Reaching out his hands the captain grasped each of his subordinates by a shoulder, giving them a hearty squeeze. "We're ready for this and so are the men; we've trained for years and now the time is come. If we meet not again tomorrow..."

"...then we will meet again in the last battle," intoned the others.

With a last nod they each turned away to gather their men; the attack was on.

# Chapter Three

Three more quiet steps and the hunter froze; ears piqued for the slightest hint of danger. An arrow remained on the string and half the slack had already been taken but the hunter had no confidence in the missile's ability to help him; he wasn't being stalked by a normal beast.

Another step forward was followed by another pause; the hunter knew better than to move in the same pattern every time; that made it too easy for someone following you to do so silently. Another step, a pause, and then six in rapid succession brought neither sounds of crashing brush nor the scent of a carnivore to his nostrils. Had he lost the beast? The hunter doubted it; this type of creature wasn't so easily fooled. Not even the Keon-din could conceal his trail from a Were.

Kog was a young Quarg; barely blooded in his people's eyes but he was good in the forest; good enough to be named a full tracker. He had been very proud of his accomplishment and had led a group of warriors out to search for human hunters believed to be in the area. Now all those warriors were dead and only he survived.

It had not been his fault but the chief of his tribe wouldn't see it that way. Not that the chief's displeasure wasn't something to be avoided, but right now a beating would seem like paradise if Kog could only escape from the Were to receive it.

His only chance was if the beast had stopped to feed; the bodies of the five slain warriors were enough to keep its attention if it were a mere animal. Kog had met several Weres in the great camp and knew them to be smart. However most were cruel and wouldn't let anything survive their attack; particularly if they didn't want the other Weres to know that they were killing Quargs. Kog knew his duty; to return to camp and warn his chief, who would in turn warn Handrick, the Were who led them.

A branch snapped and Kog's blood froze. Turning his head slowly, his heart pounding so quickly he was afraid it might burst, the young Quarg's worst fears were realized; standing not twenty paces away stood a nightmare.

The creature's fur was brown save for a strip of black that ran down its chest. It was tall, standing as it was in its half-human, half-wolf form; taller than Kog by a head or more despite a slight stoop. Kog got the sense that the Were was young, perhaps even his own age, but it was muscular and had a snout full of long teeth. Fresh blood coated its lower jaw and neck; proof that it had indeed fed on the fresh Quarg kills it had made. As Weres go, it was only remarkable for two things; one was the thick foam dripping from its muzzle and the second was the arm that was missing just below the elbow.

Responding as he had been trained Kog spun and fired his arrow point-blank then ran as fast as he could in the opposite direction. Laughingly the Were slapped the arrow away, the terrified Quarg had failed to pull the bowstring back very far even if the Were's flesh could have been penetrated by such a weapon, and began an easy lope after his latest prey.

Kog churned his legs, bursting onto the trail he had been paralleling and immediately reaching his top speed. Behind him the Were picked up the pace, surprised at the sheer speed the Quarg was able to achieve. The chase went on for some distance, with the terrified Quarg slowly gaining ground and showing no sign of exhaustion. Finally the Were realized that it was about to lose this particular prey so the bestial man transformed further between one running step and another, taking the full wolf form in mid stride to increase its speed; and promptly crashing to his face on the trail as the missing leg was not there to take his weight. Scrambling back to its feet the Were limped as quickly as it could but soon realized that it would not be able to catch the Quarg.

Kog never once looked back, but ran all the way to his tribe's camp convinced that the Were was but one step behind.

# Chapter Four

The first sign of civilization was a disappointment. The farm house was old and had been abandoned for years; even the moss-covered walls of the stone well had collapsed but Jamus chose to be optimistic, believing that the building had been deserted because a better had been built and not that every soul in the area had been ruthlessly slaughtered.

Leaning into the straps he tugged the travois on past the farm, gratified to see that the dim track he followed appeared to be widening slightly. Soon he began passing fields that, while fallow now that the harvest was past, had obviously been worked recently. Low stone walls appeared, none higher than his knee, to separate one field from another and Jamus eagerly scanned the horizon for the smoke of cook fires. He didn't have long to wait.

"Come along now," he wheezed to his unconscious passengers. "We'll soon be warm again and I'll have something decent to wear." Jamus didn't bother looking back; he knew neither could hear him.

Snow had fallen through the night but thankfully hadn't amounted to much. As noon passed, so did the last of the snow, and the temperature rose slightly with the sun. His sense of smell had returned abruptly, much to his chagrin when he caught a sniff of himself, and the illness he had been expecting to claim him after sleeping outside again had never arrived.

The last few hours Jamus had spent talking to his unconscious passengers as he drug the travois, worried that he might be delirious. But once he realized that the talking seemed to make his struggles more bearable he continued, speaking of many things as the day drug by. Had either been awake to listen, they would have learned a great deal about the pampered Viscount, particularly when it came to his relationship with his wife.

Each time he stopped to rest, which was far too often he knew, the Viscount would spend the time listening for any sign of the Were he had heard yesterday. His night had been spent in abject certainty that the beast would pounce upon him from the darkness at any moment; carefully choosing him from among his companions for its meal as he would choose a rare steak over cold mutton. One would have to surmise that the nobility tasted better, it only made sense from a dietary point of view if not the preferred breeding. So far he had heard nothing of any prowling beasts, at least not while he was in the forest. Since he had left the shelter of the trees the singing of birds had returned and he dared to begin hoping that they had indeed escaped.

During his next rest break he again checked on the wounded, finding both much as they had been before. The big woodsman's wound still showed no sign of infection and Gran continued to mumble in her sleep about hoeing cabbages. Jamus couldn't imagine how either still lived but he was grateful in a way; his wife had given her life to protect Gran and it seemed like a terrible offense to him that the old woman should linger but a few more days and then die as well. Gran had to live or Eldena would have died for nothing.

"And even then, she may have," Jamus mumbled, looking upon the wrinkled old crone. He didn't even like Gran, but his wife certainly had.

"She's special Jamus, that I am certain of," Eldena had told him the night after the 'fight' between her and Gran. "My magic can't tell me exactly why, but I've never encountered anyone like her."

Jamus realized that he was crying again but noticed that no tears were falling. Shuddering in distaste he lifted one of the woodsman's shoes and took a drink of the foul water before sharing the rest with the others. Neither person stirred so he lifted the travois poles and struggled on. He had just finished telling the story of his and Eldena's first meeting, for at least the third time that day, when he saw the smoke.

Holding his breath he studied the thin, lazy trail for a moment until he was certain it was from a chimney and not the last swirls of smoke from a burned-out home. Assured he moved on, gratified to see that the lane he followed was curving just ahead, turning in the direction of the smoke. Only a thin line of trees and the shoulder of a slight rise concealed the dwelling from him now.

First the chimney came into view, then a sizeable barn beyond it. Finally Jamus completed the curve and saw the home itself; small, dreary, surely no more than a dozen rooms in total across both floors, Jamus was glad to see that at least it wasn't as small as the abandoned hovel he had just passed. As farmers go this fellow might indeed be well-off but to the Viscount the man was obviously a coinless beggar.

"Hallo the house," Jamus tried to shout but his lack of breath caused it to come out as nothing more than a wheeze. He need not have worried, as some of the denizens of the farm were already aware of his presence.

Like ghosts they appeared here and there among the trees, two even came up behind him. They were long-legged and lean, looking half-starved, and bared their pointed fangs in a silent snarl as the dogs gathered about him. Once they had him surrounded the largest of the pack began to bark, an action picked up by the others until the din was so loud Jamus could no longer hear himself saying "nice doggie, good boy."

"Ho Fang, down Ralf," shouted a voice from the direction of the barn. A moment later a boy of about sixteen poked a head out of the loft. "Just stay where you are and they won't bite. We'll be down in a moment."

Jamus bit off his retort, barely, concerning where the boy thought he might be going when surrounded by killer hounds, and bid his time trying not to lift his gaze from his own feet. The dogs were not so reticent, and despite the boy's promise eased closer, tightening their ring step by stiff-legged step.

"That's enough Bitsy," stated a deeper voice. Risking a glance to his left Jamus saw an older man standing atop the rise, a bow with readied arrow in his hands. Another man, this one no more than twenty, stepped from the brush to Jamus' left whispering to the dogs. He was armed only with a wooden pitchfork but the dogs immediately sat when he approached. Soon the ring of dogs was encircled by another ring, this one of farmers dressed similarly in woolen homespun and armed with a variety of implements including hoes and one young woman even brandishing the handle out of a butter churn.

"You're not welcome here son," stated the man with the bow. Taking a quick glance around at the angry faces of the farmers, Jamus certainly had to agree.

# Chapter Five

Gotag stomped angrily along the forest trail, trying in vain to stamp down his temper along with the nearly-frozen dirt. He was a great warrior, the best from his tribe in generations, or so his mother had told him. To be sent out to hunt while most of his fellows were storming the human palace was too much of an insult to be ignored but he did not yet have enough status as a warrior to challenge those in authority. Not yet, at least. So now he had to pursue the soft lowland deer rather than grow rich off the plunder of a king.

To his left moved three of his tribesmen, to the right four more. They were trying, so far in vain, to scare up some type of game to help feed the gathered horde. Coming towards them were a dozen wolves the Quargs were hoping to drive the prey to. It was a more efficient way to hunt the large quantity of game they needed but it still served as an added insult for Gotag; he was to be denied even the simple pleasure of killing the prey himself.

The soft warble of the mountain thrush, imitated very badly, brought Gotag to one knee, a fist held high to signal the others. He looked first to his right and saw nothing but expectant faces among those Quargs, so he looked back to his left to find his cousin Vilex waving an arm slowly to gain his attention. Catching Gotag's eye, Vilex held up a finger, then spread his hand wide, and then pointed ahead.

One prey, large in size, and it was somewhere to their front. Gotag remained where he was, searching the bare branches of the bracken for the prey Vilex had seen. The ground sloped off gently where he was but became steeper just ahead, dropping off into another of the sinkholes the area was filled with. At first he saw nothing and then, from the corner of his eye, caught a brief glimpse of movement; it was right where Vilex had indicated.

Perhaps he was going to see something bleed today after all. He placed an arrow across the string of his bow and watched as the other Quargs followed suit. Rising to his feet he began to ease forward as silently as he was able, his bow bent and arrow ready to fly as he watched for any further sign of the prey. If he saw any hint of movement, he intended to release his arrow on the off-chance he might get lucky firing through the undergrowth. If he missed, at least one of the others wouldn't.

Just then another bit of movement caught his attention; across the sinkhole and up the ridge; well above his present position. Focusing on the spot he recognized one of their wolves, an old gray she-wolf Gotag himself had hand raised. She was down on her belly, slinking along as she stalked whatever it was that hid in the thicket. Unwilling to share his kill Gotag made a sudden decision, and leapt forward at full speed down the slope, not giving the command to attack until he had a half-dozen step lead on the other Quargs. Trained to react to the same command, the wolves appeared all along the far slope and rushed in as well but Gotag was happy to see that neither Quarg nor wolf would reach the prey before him.

Was it a deer? Perhaps a bear? Gotag would be content to kill even a mok but knew that they were unlikely to be about at this time of the day. He'd gladly kill anything at the moment, just to ease the resentment he felt at being excluded from the battle. He crashed through the first wave of brambles pretending that they were the walls the humans built around their villages and stormed ahead screaming a war cry he had invented himself; great warriors were known to do that. At first he saw nothing but then he spied a glimpse of brown fur just beyond a fallen log. Skidding to a halt Gotag barely aimed before he fired, but knew instantly that his shot was true.

And then the arrow bounced off the target.

Snarling to himself Gotag scrambled for a second arrow, mentally declaring revenge against whoever was responsible for ruining his shot. Had someone filed his points down? It had happened before; everyone was jealous of him. Before he could set the new arrow to the string the beast arose to its full height and gave a snarl of defiance.

Skidding hard the other Quargs stopped their forward progress, two by slipping on the frozen mud beneath the wet leaves and falling to their backsides. The wolves immediately dropped to their haunches and tucked their tails between their legs as the Were came into sight.

"What are you doing here... sir?" Gotag stammered, quickly lowering his bow and allowing the arrow to fall from his fingertips. All the Weres were supposed to be either taking the palace or away plundering the city of Aldrigal.

The Were snarled again, standing protectively over the carcass it was feeding on. Whatever it was lay hidden behind the log, but Gotag could see the fresh blood on the creature's snout.

"We apologize for interrupting your meal," the Quarg offered, trying to back up the slope without taking his eyes off the Were. "We didn't know you were hunting here, we'll try somewhere else."

This time the Were didn't reply, just squatted slightly as if returning to its meal. Gotag took that opportunity to turn around and hurry, certainly not run because great warriors didn't run, as he retreated to the protection of his fellows who, one by one, were gathering together near where Gotag had entered the thicket.

"What's he doing here," growled a particularly stupid Quarg named Nod.

"He's still looking at us," whispered Vilex. "Why don't he go back to eating?"

The last Quarg of the hunting party joined them then and asked, "Did you see what he's eating?"

"Deer? A bear? What difference does it make?" demanded another.

"It was the wrong color for a bear, it had to be a mok or something," stated Gotag, remembering a brief glimpse of darker fur he had seen on the carcass when the Were stood up.

"That wasn't no mok, but I think it was wearing a mok-fur coat," whispered the late arrival, the blood draining from his face.

"A mok-fur coat?" replied Nod, who still didn't understand what the others had already gotten.

"Wasn't Sar-tob wearing a mok-fur coat?" another Quarg asked, matching the quiet tone of voice all but Nod had by now adopted.

"Sar-tob is a traitor and a coward," snarled Nod. "All know he deserted yesterday."

"I don't think he deserted, Nod, and keep your voice down," urged Gotag, lightly cuffing the other Quarg to gain his attention. "I think that Were is eating him."

"And if he hears us talking about it, he might come after us," whined Vilex.

"I don't know if he's even listening," stated Gotag, risking a quick glance at the Were. "But he sure is watching us."

"He don't look right, not like the others."

"I don't remember seeing him in the big camp, he must be new."

"I agree with Crod," whispered Vilex. "He doesn't look right somehow. Not smart like the others."

"Maybe it's that one from the road."

"That was a rumor."

"Lag-tard said it was true, and he was there," argued Vilex with the doubter.

"Let's get out of here," added another Quarg, even as the group began to move together back the way they had come. Even Nod came along without a long pause like he usually needed before making even the simplest of decisions.

"Somebody whistle for the wolves," ordered Gotag quietly.

"Whistle for them yourself," scoffed Vilex. "I don't want to attract any more attention to myself."

The Were left the shelter of his log, took a dozen long strides and then easily leaped over the Quargs, twisting as he did so to land in a crouch facing them.

Starting, some of the Quargs whimpered in fear as they all cowered before the beast. Gotag dredged up enough courage to address it.

"Uh... yes sir, can we help you?" he squeaked. Afraid to look the creature in the eyes Gotag instead concentrated on the beast's muzzle but that didn't help as the sight of the long blood-stained fangs and a hint of white foam gathered between them frightened him even more.

"Look, one of his arms is missing," whispered Nod.

"Yeah, and its eyes... they look... wrong," muttered Vilex.

The Were continued to ignore them, at least it did not reply, and remained in its crouch; knees deeply bent and arm placed on the ground before it. Its belly was distended from feeding; it had obviously eaten well, and Gotag had time to be glad that the creature wasn't hungry.

In a blur of movement the Were exploded from its crouch and clamped its teeth onto Vilex's throat. It gave the Quarg a quick shake and then dropped him, leaping onto Nod who stood frozen with surprise and fear. The other Quargs immediately broke away from their cluster, scattering in all directions. A few tried to draw their feeble weapons as they ran but most didn't bother; they all knew they had no chance of even wounding the Were with anything they carried.

Gotag threw his bow down and ran back into the thicket, catching sight of a well-chewed Quarg body as he leaped over the log. Someone screamed off to his left but he didn't pause; his only thought now was escape. Hopefully the others would keep the Were busy enough that he could slip away.

Around him the wolves ran too, trailing him or trotting along side through the trees. He felt some comfort in their presence but still had no thought concerning fighting the Were; the wolves would have no better chance than he did but at least they too might slow it down.

Gotag crested the next rise and found the trail dropping again just as another scream sounded from somewhere behind him. The sound of water told of a stream, he could just see the glint of water flowing between this hill and the next, and he allowed himself to pick up whatever momentum he could as he ran towards it. When he reached the water he ran along side it until his momentum slowed but he kept on; leaping from rock to fallen log and from bank to bank as he avoided the steep hillsides and followed the path of least resistance. Finally he could run no more and collapsed in the water itself beneath an overhang the water had carved from a bank.

Almost immediately the old gray she-wolf and two others trotted into sight and joined him, the she dropping to her haunches and whining at him. She was afraid too, but Gotag didn't take the time to comfort her; he had to regain his wind so that he could run some more.

His breathing slowed but the pounding of his heart refused to do so. Eventually, after hearing yet another dying scream from back upstream, Gotag decided that he had to move on. The Were had plenty of targets but was obviously not killing to feed; it was killing to prevent their returning to report it or, even worse, was simply killing for the mindless joy of it. Another pair of wolves joined them as he rested, and two more just as he stood up to continue his run. He had already begun concocting a tall tale in his mind to tell of his bravery; hadn't he stayed behind to gather up the wolves when the others ran?

Gotag walked for a while, staying in the streambed to hide his scent, until his feet were numb from the icy water. When he finally dared he stepped onto a rock and used it to propel himself onto the left-hand bank and then he began to jog, the wolves running before and behind, switching sides of the narrow stream with long leaps as necessary to find the best footing. He jogged until he began to feel tired again, the hope of escape just beginning to dawn before he saw the wolves stopping in their tracks.

Skidding to a halt, nearly slipping back into the stream when his feet skidded on the remnants of last summer's moss, Gotag dropped to a crouch and began studying in his surroundings. The stream still ran steeply downward before him and the hills to either hand had grown noticeably higher from his descent. A deadfall to his right limited his view in that direction so after a quick glance to the left he concentrated on the deadfall, and so had a clear view when the Were leapt to the top of the log.

Rigid with fear Gotag didn't bother to run, or even make a move to defend himself until the Were stalked closer. And closer it came; still in its half-man form it took long, careful steps after dropping from the log; almost as if it expected the Quarg to run and was anticipating the pleasure of chasing him down. Finally, with only the narrow stream itself between them, Gotag found a small measure of courage and did the only thing his desperate mind could think of; he whistled for the wolves.

Obediently they came at his call, but with ears down and tails tucked. They gathered around the stream whining in confusion; looking as if they expected to be beaten at any second. They were his only hope; a minor distraction at best. Gotag gathered his courage, pointed at the Were and gave the command.

"Kill," he ordered, then turned and began to run once again. He passed two wolves slinking towards the Were and a small hope began to grow; a hope squashed when the Were's claws pierced the flesh of his shoulder.

Gotag's last thoughts were not fear, or even pain, but confusion as the old gray she-wolf watched him being thrown to the ground and mauled without responding. His eyes clouded over while focused on her.

The one-armed Were made quick work of the Quarg and, since it had already fed, left the corpse where it fell when the last signs of life were gone. Looking at the closest wolf, the old she, the Were locked gazes with the animal for a long moment before lifting his muzzle into the air, sniffing deeply for the scent of new prey.

Grunting once, the Were moved back uphill in the direction he had come; a line of wolves trailing obediently after.

# Chapter Six

Ordering the men to keep silent the Captain led them through the back allies searched so diligently the past week. Unlike their countrymen in the First Light Foot, the men of the second had not had the luxury of staying in inns and taverns, but had instead spent their days cramped up in the basements of homes and businesses owned or under the direct influence of the Duke of Firth. They were glad just to leave the cramped confines and get out into the open air. They were close now; close enough to see the Merchant Quarter gate if not for the building they now sheltered behind.

The Second Firthian Light Foot had the more difficult challenge. The seasoned mercenaries of the Merchants Quarter were experienced and well paid. This did not, however, make them particularly brave when outnumbered; or at least the Captain of the Second hoped so.

The alley they were in was wide, as alleys go, and the one that opened within sight of the gate was wider still. With this many men gathered here, it was crowded; even more so since the warriors of the Second were clustered as far from the Signaler as possible.

Emaciated to the utmost, the woman did nothing to enhance her appearance. Her red hair was cut short randomly, as if she did it herself with a knife and no mirror. Her face was scarred with the marks of some pox or plague and her clothing; faded purple pants missing one leg below the knee and a yellow shirt overtopped with a grease-stained cotton apron, did not match and were woefully inadequate for the weather. If the Signaler was suffering from the bitter cold she wasn't showing it. Only the Captain stood near her and it took a supreme effort of his will to do so.

Signaling to his junior officers, a pair of Calques where most units had but one, the Captain motioned for them to join him. Standing in a semi-circle the three officers clustered together with the Signaler facing them; no one wanted to actually stand by her and it wasn't only her odor that urged them away; she stared at them with bulging eyes that rarely blinked caused a small part in their avoidance but the main element was the way the hackles rose on their necks when near her.

"Bring them up; first squad to the left, second to the right, the rest through here," the Captain ordered in soft tones. The buildings around them were well-to-do shops rather than homes but it was always possible that an apprentice might be sleeping in an upper room. "Have everyone double time once they leave the alleys but remind them to be as quiet as possible; we don't want to alert the guards any sooner than necessary."

"Your men will not be heard," intoned the Signaler, her goggle-eyes lifting to focus briefly on the Captain. "I have seen to it."

Repressing a shiver the Captain replied, "Thank you, but I still want the men to maintain their discipline."

The Senior Calque cleared his throat, unwilling to speak up in front of the Signaler without his Captain's nod. "We lead the squads up the stairs to clear the wall while you take the gatehouse."

"Then I will signal my sisters," added the Signaler, feeling somewhat more talkative than usual. Her voice didn't match her appearance; it was very high pitched and melodious. The Captain had often thought that she might have a pleasant singing voice but there was no way that he wanted to hear any song she might want to sing.

"Any questions?" the Captain asked. No one replied so he nodded to his officers and sent them back to their squads.

As he was pledged to do the Captain was the first man to leave the night's shadows gathered in the alley and emerge on the wide cobblestone plaza that fronted the Merchant's Gate. As the defenses had been designed to keep attackers out, the stairs that accessed the walls as well as the doors into the gatehouse itself were open before them even though the gate itself was closed for the night. Jogging as silently as he could the Captain listened for the telltale jingling or muffled thumps that this many men would have to create. The skin of his back crawled when he heard nothing; absolutely nothing. It was too cold for insects but he found himself praying to at least hear the chirp of a cricket.

They crossed the plaza and the Captain lost sight of his Calques as they led their men up the stairs. No lights were showing in the gatehouse and no guards appeared to raise a cry at their approach. Nearly dizzy with their early success the Captain reached the stone door that led to the gate winch. And there found no handle, merely a small window that opened from the inside.

Things always went wrong in a plan as detailed as this, and this was likely only the first setback they would suffer. Pausing only a moment to decide what course to follow, the Captain allowed his choices to flow through his mind. Break it down? Too noisy, despite the Signaler's claims of silence. Send runners up to the walls and look for a way down? The Calques would do that anyway if the walls fell before the gatehouse and having two squads of men standing here in the open waiting would eventually bring unwanted attention. His musings were interrupted when a thin hand was placed on his arm.

Stepping to his side the Signaler thrust one hand into a pocket of her apron, a lip curling up in preparation for the magic she had in mind. The Captain felt a lump of fear crop up in his throat at the thought of what a blast powerful enough to open the door would do to the men beginning to cluster about; or the noise and light it would have to produce. Swallowing his fear, and his distaste at touching her, the Captain grabbed her shoulder and gently pushed her aside. The time might come when her way was necessary but there were other options to try first. With her out of the way, the Captain rapped sharply on the door.

"You're supposed to knock twice, then wait," growled a voice from beyond the portal, the words the only precursor to the sound of a metal bar being pulled back. Surprised, the Captain pushed the door open and followed it into the gatehouse, meeting the eyes of an even more surprised man.

"My apologies, my friend," the Captain said, placing the point of his sword beneath the man's chin and leading him gently to one side of the door, allowing his men to pour through after him.

Three other men were in the gatehouse but all were asleep; a big fire roaring in a brazier across the room. All were taken without a struggle. Men hurried up the stairs to the room above and after the sound of a single blow of sword on sword, all went silent there.

"Captain, the gatehouse is secured," reported a trooper from the top of the stairs. Reeling at the ease of it all the Captain turned his prisoner over to another soldier and nodded to the Signaler.

"It's your turn now."

Smiling the Signaler stalked up the stairs, her hands held wide as if moving to embrace a loved one; her face joyous. The Captain followed behind, needlessly motioning for his soldiers to move out of her way. Upon reaching the second floor the officer spared but a single glance, finding more gate guards being held prisoner; one with a bleeding scalp. His people looked fine so he continued to follow the Signaler up a rusty iron ladder bolted to one wall and through an iron trapdoor to the roof of the gatehouse.

As the Signaler whispered to herself the Captain took a long look in all directions; there was a fire to the south but the Merchants Quarter remained quiet. His men were in place along the walls, so the other squads had had no more trouble than he had in taking the gatehouse.

"You should leave now, get below," growled the Signaler, her eyes closed and her shoulders trembling slightly.

Feeling a presence in the air he didn't like, the Captain took the opportunity to flee the rooftop, taking the time to close the trapdoor behind him just in time to avoid the worst of the flash of light.

# Chapter Seven

"State your name, stranger," said the deep voice. He was the oldest of those gathered and looked like he could be the father or grandfather of the others.

"My name is...Jamus," he replied, suddenly deciding not to reveal his nobility. The peasantry, particularly those so far from the larger cities and active nobles, were sometimes vengeful to their betters.

"What happened to your friends?" interrupted the woman with the butter churn handle. "They ain't feverish, Randle, they've been hurt," she declared, tucking the handle through a loop on her belt and kicking her way through the dogs to the side of the travois.

The change over the others was marked, as weapons were lowered or disappeared completely as the now concerned farmers rushed forward to view the injured. Jamus watched as the end of the travois holding Gran and the woodsman was lifted by a pair of young men and drug at a full run towards the house with the farmers jogging along behind, leaving him with the now friendly dogs and the older man with the bow.

"Sorry stranger, but you can't be too careful. Fever took root over to Plowdale last year and one in three died," the man explained as he gingerly worked his way down the slope. "We seen you coming down the trail and figured you people were fleeing the plague or worse."

"I'm afraid it's worse," muttered Jamus. "Quargs are rampaging along the main road and we barely escaped..." he choked up. "My wife..."

Randle clapped a hand on Jamus' shoulder. "No need to say anything more, stranger. We understand death around here."

Jamus took a few more steps as he regained his composure. "Where are we?"

Randle shrugged. "Doesn't really have a name. This is my farm; I'm a freeman. My father earned this little plot of ground in service to the King of Aldrigal. There's a village that way," he waved further down the trail Jamus had been following, "called Vicksville."

Never having heard of the village Jamus instead concentrated on the fact that they were still within the nominal borders of Aldrigal.

"Who is the nearest nobleman? We have to warn them about the Quargs," he asked, initially reluctant to share the existence of the Were, or Weres, to this simple farmer.

"There isn't any; we call this area Freeman's Green. It's only barely in Aldrigal, and was once part of the Cafalstic Empire. Once that little bit of trouble was over Aldrigal wasn't the only nation to claim it, so we Freemen were given land here to reinforce the King's claim. No one thought we would be able to hold on without royal support but since the King had nothing to lose, he gave us the chance."

"Then who organizes local defenses against the Quargs?"

Randle shrugged. "Mostly we do it ourselves; each farm is pretty well defended and the village has a wall around it. We get about one Quarg raid a year and have to do what we can to defend ourselves. If we have any warning, we move the youngsters and old people into town and retreat there ourselves when it gets bad enough. We've been burned out twice."

"Then you should probably get your people together; we should all get behind those walls as soon as possible; its not just Quargs coming this time."

"Now stranger..."

"Jamus."

"Right, Jamus. And my name is Randle. We'll give up our home when we have to, but not before. We'll see to your people, get you some clothes, and get you fed while some of my grandsons scout back along your trail. Then we'll decide what we need to do."

Grabbing the older man's arm Jamus forced him to turn to meet his eyes. The old farmer was thin but strong; his muscles felt like iron beneath the Viscount's fingers.

"You have to understand, there's more out there than Quargs!"

"We know about the wolves, Jamus. Quargs and their pets are no strangers to us."

"Not just wolves, Randle, but wolves the size of ponies! And that's not all; the Quargs are being led by something worse, far worse."

"Son what are you saying?"

"Weres, Randle. The forest is full of Weres!"

Now it was Randle's turn to grab Jamus by the arm. "What do you mean, boy. Do those that are with you carry the Curse?" he demanded, no sign of kindness in his voice now. "What have you brought down on us?"

Jamus didn't even try to pull his arm free but met the taller man's gaze. "They are not Cursed and neither am I. We escaped by chance when, I believe, two of the Weres began fighting among themselves. The old woman hit her head and the man took a Quarg arrow, that's all."

The farmer's next words were interrupted when a woman came to the door of the house; her voice carried worry that broke through the man's emotions.

"Pa, you need to come in here now."

Releasing Jamus, Randle hurried, as much of a run as his old, thin legs could produce. Jamus followed along despite the look the woman gave him; what could she possibly have against him? She didn't yet know about the Weres.

The walls of the home were of whole logs above a fieldstone foundation that came up as high as Jamus' waist He immediately noticed that the second and third floors hung out beyond the bottom; like a stairway in reverse. Loopholes looked down from each overhang, allowing defenders to fire missiles down on anyone trying to approach the walls. The door was thick and made of oak slabs reinforced with iron bands and was approached by a set of steps made again of stone. Stepping into the house Jamus thought to find a wooden floor as well, but found stones beneath his feet; was the house setting upon a large pile of stones? The first floor of the home was one large room, with a huge open fireplace in the center and a long table lined with more than a dozen chairs. There were no windows at all and the room was dark despite several lanterns and the glow of the cheery fire. The dogs followed them in and collapsed around the room.

"This isn't a farmhouse, it's a castle," Jamus thought to himself.

The farmer stood beside the travois, which had been brought directly into the house and left near the fire. Blankets and furs had been heaped nearby and Gran placed upon them. Another pile stood ready, but the woodsman remained atop the travois. It was over him that Randle stood with a circle of his family. In all there were at least two dozen adults in the room and at least that many small children. Most of the latter were clustered in groups in the far corners, away from the strangers and their odd smells.

The warmth of the fire struck Jamus like a blow and his body began to shiver uncontrollably. Someone helped him to a chair as those gathered continued to speak.

"He's an outlaw," whispered the woman who had previously been armed with the butter-churn handle. "You recognize him the same as I do."

"He'll fetch a sizeable reward," whistled a man of middle-age. Jamus didn't remember him from the road.

"Who are you people?" demanded a younger man.

"We're not turning him in; that's the man that saved Saree," argued a woman of about twenty.

"Stole her right out of a Quarg camp and brought her home," agreed a man with silver at his temples.

"Yes and then stole all the money old Wildebur had hid under his floorboard," offered an older woman.

Randle snorted. "We don't know that he did that."

"He must have," the woman argued. "He's a criminal; just look at the size of the reward on his head."

"Burt's got a reward on his head, from that trip up to Aldrigal City that time," laughed a youth. "I'm all for turning him in."

"We don't know that he's done anything," stated Randle.

"He saved Saree, and that's something that we know," rejoined the silver-templed man.

"Not quick enough, though. The Quargs had already had her five days. For all we know they just got tired of her and gave her to this one to bring her back home," snorted the older woman.

"Naw, Ma, them Quargs, they would have just eaten Saree if they were done with her," argued the youth.

"Like you'd know," growled an older youth that, by his reactions to the earlier jibes was probably the one named Burt, punctuating his words by shoving the younger man.

"She ain't been the same since neither," argued a thin man with a beard that nearly reached his waist. He looked enough like Randle to be a grandson. "But she always spoke highly of this feller," he finished, waving a hand over the unconscious woodsman.

"No one is turning anyone in, not until I figure out what is going on here," stated Randle and everyone stopped arguing and broke up the gathering. Randle continued speaking, giving orders enough to keep everyone busy, then went back outside with a herd of his kinsmen.

As some of the women worked over Gran and the woodsman was transferred to a pile of blankets, others tended several large cooking pots and a boy of ten brought a thick blanket to drape over Jamus. Still shivering the viscount could do nothing but nod once in appreciation as he trembled.

"Naw, now don't do that," a woman stated, jerking the blanket from his shaking fingers. "Don't block off the heat of the fire, just wear it like this," she said, draping it loosely over his shoulders. Too feeble to fight, Jamus merely closed his eyes and soaked up the heat.

Perhaps an hour passed as Jamus slowly regained control of himself. Once his shaking subsided he was brought clothing; simple, homespun attire similar to what everyone else was wearing. Unashamedly he stripped off his silk loin cloth to pull the others on. One little girl giggled but no one else seemed to notice. He carefully slipped his little money from the ruins of his loincloth and into the pocket of his new trousers. Once he had retaken his seat a cup of broth was brought to him, thick with cubes of mutton and tiny chunks of carrots, and after he had sipped that for a while a pitcher of water and a tin cup. The warmth of the broth was wonderful but he found himself drinking several cups of the cold water in quick succession. How much better it tasted without the leather shoe/sweaty foot flavoring!

Just as he finished off the last of the broth the door burst open and a crowd of excited young men followed Randle into the home. Cuffing the nearest of the boys the old man managed to silence them enough to be heard. Everyone in the room was looking at him intently and not a sound could be heard save the soft snoring of the woodsman. Randle's eyes were frightened but his words were simple.

"Pack up all we can easily carry; we're all going to town."

# Chapter Eight

The Were that once was Albrim continued to track down and kill lone Quargs as he found them. No memory of who and what he once was remained within his bestial brain; he simply found the scent of Quargs familiar and by now knew them to be easy prey.

Unlike the wolves that followed him the Were did not hunt only for food but rather for the joy of killing itself. Rarely did he bother to feed on his prey; there were simply too many about to bother. His pack fed well and their numbers grew daily as he moved about the forest, gathering all the wolves that came within his influence. So far as his limited imagination could understand he was the ruler of all.

Frustrated by his missing arm the Were was unable to utilize his more comfortable wolf-like form for hunting and traveling. Forced to spend most of his time in the half-wolf half-man form caused him pain. This made him irritable and only fanned the killing rage he slaked on everything that crossed his path or passed him upwind. All except the wolves; for them he had no anger and, though he didn't understand it, was pleased to have them nearby. Only when he rested was he able to alter himself to his more natural wolf form. At least his sleep was without pain.

His mind was focused on the thoughts of his pack-mates as he carefully sniffed along the path for the scent of prey. Most of those he hunted kept to the cleared places and Albrim had begun to search them out. He didn't understand that the places where the earth shown through the vegetation were paths, but he did understand that his prey could be found on them; which was perfectly fine with him; it only made their scent easier to follow. Albrim also did not understand the lure of water to his prey, he could not bear to drink fresh water, but he had learned that prey sought it out and so he occasionally rested near such places, simply to wait.

His pack mates sent images to him; of rabbits sleeping in their burrows, of mok hibernating, of deer hiding through the day in their thickets; but no scent of anything else. The Were disdained such easy prey; only deer were a challenge and he was unable to chase them down. Bear would be better, or some of the larger beasts he had already discovered could be found in this area, but nothing had been found this day. No problem; he would continue to search.

Walking doubled over so his nose remained as close to the ground as possible, Albrim trotted along the trail towards the nearest spring. He knew where it was; he'd killed a Quarg there only yesterday. He was almost there when he heard the excited howl of one of his pack.

He sent a question through their connection; a simply query though wordless. "What have you found?"

The thoughts came flooding back; two-legs, walking upright, a pack of them. To a wolf more than a pair were a pack, but to Albrim's slightly more intelligent mind he discerned that there were more than the digits on his forepaw.

Almost he gave the signal for the pack to follow. Almost he didn't take the few seconds necessary to complete his path to the edge of the spring. Almost.

The smell was faint but there. The new prey had passed by the spring sometime during the night. Far stronger prey than the bipeds his pack mates had found had drunk of the water before moving on.

"To me! To me!" he bellowed, lifting his voice to the heavens as he also gave the mental command. Here was strong prey! Here was the test he needed! Now he needed only to track it down.

One by one the wolves gathered to him and he waited for them all before he moved. They would be of no use in the coming battle; even the bestial Albrim understood that, but he wanted them with him to witness his great victory; to share in his triumph! His heart full of joy he howled again, straining his lungs as his pack mates joined him in his call. Hopefully the prey was close enough to hear and accept his challenge. This day Albrim would pursue his greatest prey; this day he was tracking another Were.

# Chapter Nine

"Get in here, Randle," yelled the man atop the wooden gates.

Below him the gates of Vicksville were standing open for the citizens of Freeman's Green to enter. They formed a long, moving line of refugees coming from all directions for the hopeful safety of the stout timber walls that surrounded the town. Most looked hopeful, some even looked joyful as they contemplated a few days away from farm work spent in the pleasures to be found in a town of nearly a thousand.

Randle waved from his seat atop the wagon; behind him were piles of blankets, barrels of preserves, and somehow wedged between it all, Gran and Mute. Other wagons came behind them carrying the farmer's two-dozen-odd descendants and accumulated in-laws, along with as many supplies as they could carry. Flocks of sheep were being driven along to either side with the dogs doing most of the work there.

"Be along in a few, Lauder, and you're buying," Randle bellowed.

The man above the gate smiled but he didn't look pleased. He waved once more and disappeared from view.

"Who was that?" asked Jamus from his seat beside the farmer.

"That's Lauder; he's the mayor of Vicksville and a good friend. Used to be a farmer but his back went bad on him," Randle laughed. "If the truth be known he was a poor farmer, and complained about his back when he was still a lad. I think he's just lazy."

Jamus said nothing to that; he often used claims of back pain to avoid the rare bits of strenuous exercise others tried to thrust upon him.

"Now he makes barrels; went to Aldrigal and learned how. He never apprenticed to anyone, but he watched them enough to learn the basics," Randle turned about and thumped a barrel with the palm of his hand. "They're not good barrels, but they're the only ones made nearby, so he does a good business."

"Will he be able to organize the defenses?"

"Yes and no; I served the king in my time and likely he'll lean on me more than a little about that. There are one or two others that are veterans, and they'll not be shy about stating their opinions. Lauder's a good man; he'll know when to listen and when to command."

Jamus looked at the tall logs that made up the walls. The tops were pointed but hardly more than four men in height. The walls were square and each corner held a tower again made of logs.

"But these walls are made of logs!" Jamus sputtered. "If the Weres can't climb them the Quargs can certainly burn them! You were better off in your house; at least the foundations were stone."

Randle laughed, albeit it a nervous one. "These same walls have held off Quargs since just after the Were War; they'll last a few days more I believe. And the walls may not be so high as those of Aldrigal but no Were will be climbing them any more than a Quarg can burn them. Look a little closer, boy."

Studying the logs as he had been told, Jamus noticed that they were quite dark in color and had no visible bark left on them. He was no expert on how logs aged but turning dark seemed a reasonable reaction. It wasn't until they were passing through the gates that he was close enough to notice another small detail.

"Why are they shiny?"

Randle slapped his knee. "Took you long enough to notice! Those logs have been treated with a mixture of tar, resin, maple syrup, and sap from the winter palm, along with a couple of other things they won't even tell me about, every month since they were put in the ground. They are as slick as glass and wouldn't burn if you dropped them in hellfire. Once the Quargs tore down every building and cut down every tree around and tried to build a tower big enough to go over the top of the walls, but they got tired of getting feathered by the archers on the walls. You don't have to worry about them climbing it."

"Could the wolves dig under it?"

"Not likely; the logs are actually resting an arm's length into the bedrock. They've got a deep, sweet well in there and with what's being brought in enough food to last a year or better. It would take an army with siege towers and a lot of suicidal men to get in there and we don't intend to let them. Weres or no Weres, we'll hold the town just like we always have."

They rode down the street a ways, forced to pause while sheep wandered in and out of their path. Most of the dogs had lost their interest in herding for the moment and were busy reacquainting themselves with their kindred from the town and other farms.

"What convinced you that I was telling the truth about the Weres?" Jamus asked during one long pause.

Randle spit a long line of brown juice onto the nose of a sheep before replying. "Couple of my boys back trailed you, and saw the sign. Another of my boys was out hunting and seen one himself. He didn't exactly know what it was but he knew better than to get close to it. Near as they could figure the Were they saw was tracking you, or at least traveling in the same direction. Fortunately you came somewhat round about, so they were able to cut cross-country here and there and beat the creature back to the farm. The boys all got back about the same time, so I made the decision to come here."

Jamus turned around on the seat to check on the unconscious pair. The big woodsman was still snoring and the viscount took that to be a good sign. Snoring implied a more natural sleep than whatever he had been in before. Gran had awoken once at the farmhouse, staying awake only long enough to bite one of her caregivers before fading out again. That Gran had been in some type of trouble he knew, but the fact that the large man was a wanted criminal bothered him a great deal. What if the fellow had came to and murdered him along the trail?

Finally the sheep moved again and wagon resumed its slow roll. Oxen were not the swiftest of beasts but they had no trouble pulling the overburdened wagon. Finally they reached an open area near the center of town and Randle steered their wagon into a tight cluster of similar conveyances, then watched as a swarm of people arrived to strip the wagon of oxen and contents. Jamus remained with the farmer until Gran and the woodsman were carried away as well.

"There ain't no need to be following along with them; let those that know something about healing deal with the sick," Randle proclaimed, grabbing Jamus by the elbow when he tried to follow. "You need to come with me and tell Lauder what you know; mayhap you'll remember something new you ain't told me yet."

Nodding his acceptance Jamus climbed carefully down from the wagon and trailed after Randle through the growing throng. The noise was great so they didn't talk; which was fine with Jamus who wanted to study the town.

Most of the buildings were single story, though all had stone foundations and either slate or shingled roofs. Jamus was glad to see that even those homes with some measure of wood construction were painted with the slick muck that Randle claimed was fireproof. He hoped for all their sakes that they were. A few of the buildings were taller than a single floor but most of these were barns. Only two, located across from one another near the center of town, boasted a second floor that didn't have hay hanging out of it. Large pens made by stretching ropes across dead end streets held all manner of livestock and every chicken in the kingdom seemed to have traveled here to roost. The streets were generally mud, though a few had cobblestones. The mud was nearly frozen now but in the spring it must be an impossible morass.

They walked slowly through one street and then cut through someone's barn to get ahead of the crowd. Turning right Randle led the way down a muddy side street and then cut through another building, it looked like someone's home, and emerged again near the central plaza.

"I've never seen so many people here," yelled Randle over the din. "Someone spread the word before you even got to my place, obviously, but I don't even recognize some of these folk."

Jamus nodded but didn't try to reply. His throat was getting sore, probably some disease contracted from sleeping naked on the ground in the middle of winter. He didn't recognize anyone either but didn't find that surprising; he'd never been one to cavort with the hired help.

"In here," Randle bellowed, waving the way over to one side of the street. They were approaching one of the two large structures and Jamus noticed a sign over the door proclaiming it to be the 'Greensward Inn'.

They stepped through the door to find the interior warm and dark, with only a few people scattered about the two dozen or so tables in the main room. The floor was wooden planks, which was highly preferable to dirt, and a long fireplace was roaring with flame. The scent of roasting mutton instantly assaulted Jamus' senses and his stomach growled loudly.

Winding their way through the tables Randle made his way to a rickety staircase wedged in one corner. It was built in a spiral but Jamus would have bet money that it had not been built for the inn but brought in from another building that had fallen down. Ducking nearly double they made their way up the stairs, the last step was three times the distance of the others, and found themselves in a hallway that ran the length of the building.

At least this part of the inn looked somewhat comfortable; there were numbers rendered in needlepoint hanging on each door and the walls between each were decorated with doilies or hand-painted with flowers and trees.

"Lauder will be up here," Randle said, leading the way down the hall. At the last door he knocked once before pushing his way inside.

The room was sparsely furnished but all the essentials were there; a bed with a straw-stuffed mattress, a table with a wash basin, a chair, and a poorly constructed wardrobe. A tiny bowl filled with dried flower petals sat next to the wash basin but they did little to overcome the smell of the chamber pot beneath the bed. Lauder was sitting in the chair, waiting for them.

"It's about time, I thought I was going to have to drink this myself," growled Lauder, a thick set man with drooping jowls and thinning hair. He held a bottle in his hand and two tin cups were sitting on the floor. If he was surprised by Jamus' presence he didn't show it, but filled both cups for his visitors and then kept the bottle to drink out of for himself.

Randle introduced his guest and asked him to tell what he knew. Jamus did so, leaving nothing out but his status as a noble. Lauder didn't take the news well but not as badly as Jamus had expected.

"Like Quargs aren't bad enough, nor wolves neither, now we have to deal with Weres as well!" Lauder grouched, taking a long swing from his bottle. He looked to be well on his way to an afternoon drunk.

"You don't act very surprised," offered Randle. "I would guess you've already heard about them."

Lauder took another long pull at his bottle. "Yeah, we've had refugees coming in since last night; from up to the north and west. Told us about the wolves and the Weres and that ain't all! Seems like whatever is going on is bigger than just a Quarg raid; they said whole armies are marching through the countryside, heading towards Aldrigal City."

Both men were momentarily struck silent at the news.

"Who's invading?" demanded Randle.

"No one knows, at least not anybody that's passed through here. The fellow that told me that much was lucky to have gotten away. He said he saw men, human men, on horseback."

"He must be some woodsman to have gotten that close and then escaped, particularly from all those wolves," offered Jamus.

"That or really lucky," added Randle.

"He smelled like a woodsman, so I'll go with that," stated Lauder.

"Can I speak with this woodsman? I know a little about heraldry. If he can remember a banner or standard I might be able to figure out who the invaders are," asked Jamus.

"That's fine with me, but that's not going to do us much good," snorted Lauder. "We've got Quargs to deal with, and it's probably not a coincidence that they're rampaging at the same time that a foreign army is marching through their territory."

The subject changed to talk of defenses and supplies on hand, so Jamus excused himself.

"The people I came here with, where can I find them?" he asked as he stood.

"Right across the street," replied Randle, pointing out the window.

"The town hall," added Lauder.

Randle nodded. "Yes, the town hall. It's also where we hold religious services and, in times like this, it serves as our hospital. Mostly because it has that one, big room."

"We've had over a hundred people in there upon occasion," Lauder stated proudly.

"Thank you," Jamus said. "And this fellow who told you about the invasion; do you know where I might be able to find him?"

Lauder thought hard for a moment, taking a long swig from his bottle as he did so. "No, not right off, he didn't have the coin to take a room here or in the other inn, so I would bet he's down towards the south end of town. Some of the refugees have put up tents there."

"Great, my thanks again. Do you happen to remember the man's name?"

"Indeed I do; it was my father's name as a matter of fact so it was easy for me to remember. His name is Tomo."

# Chapter Ten

Marching at a speed unnatural for a man on foot the main force of the Firthian invasion force left their last safe camp and marched through the night, reaching the edge of the forest some three miles from the main gate to Aldrigal City three hours before dawn. Their minimal cavalry screen flanked them, picking up the few stray wanderers out at such a late hour and ensuring their silence. A last few small villages were bypassed or cut through altogether; the simple folk within knew better than to leave their homes when armies were marching and the leaders of the force we not worried about anyone outrunning the troops to warn the city. At the head of the army rode a woman on horseback; a Signaler by profession.

More physically appealing than most of her sisters this particular Signaler had dark blonde hair but was every bit as emaciated. She rode atop her horse with arms spread wide and her eyes closed in bliss; the wind of her passage didn't so much as stir a single strand of her filthy hair. So long as she maintained her spell the men following in her wake would maintain their speed, and she was already taxing her reserves by the time they reached the forest's edge. Immediately behind her rode the leaders of the army.

"How long can she keep this up?" one asked not long after they stopped at their first destination. Moments later his question was answered when the Signaler rolled soundlessly from her saddle and collapsed to the forest floor.

"Guess we know," chuckled the same man uneasily.

General Handrick, commander of the army, motioned an aide forward to check on the woman. Another of her sisterhood, a brunette without even the vaguest sign of beauty, had already ridden forward to take the fallen one's place.

"She's dead, my lord," the soldier said, wiping the hand he had used to touch the Signaler on his uniform. The look of distaste on his face was almost comical but no one thought for a moment that his aversion had anything to do with her just being dead.

Her replacement took over the same stance; eyes closed, arms spread wide as she faced the lights of the city visible on the horizon. If she gave any thought or felt the slightest remorse for her fallen sister she gave no hint to those who observed. Handrick didn't bother with questions about how and why the Signalers did what they did, just so long as they accomplished what the Duke of Firth had hired them for. He didn't like them, he didn't trust them, they even made him feel uncomfortable and his blood was filled with the Curse, but they were out of his control.

"Seems like they could have switched places before the first one died," commented a mercenary. "Not that I care."

"I'm kind of glad, actually," quipped another.

"What's she doing now?" asked another.

"Supposed to be keeping us hidden from magical eyes," answered another.

"Silence," hissed their sergeant, ending the discussion.

Behind them units were approaching and spreading to the left or right as ordered by the General's aide. The men looked tired but not exhausted, and they had already traveled further this night than they otherwise could have in three days of marching.

Motioning for his senior officers to gather about him, Handrick pointedly turned his back on the living Signaler.

Handrick studied the five men. Even in the dark and in his human form his vision was superior to any human and the men's faces stood out clearly. General Intona was technically his second in command and currently sat his nervous horse to Handrick's right. A spit and polish veteran, the man demanded those under his command to maintain strict discipline at all times. The murmuring of the men in the ranks immediately behind them had the general's face red with rage. Middle aged, the general was portly and balding but exercised vigorously to maintain his weight. Hopeless as a tactician, he had been passed over for this command but was beginning to deal with it thanks to the wise handling he had received by Handrick. The man had his uses despite being nothing more than a human.

To Intona's right sat Colonel Barant; commander of the Firthian cavalry. The man typically stayed as close to Intona as he could without sharing a saddle and kept his eyes on the Weres. Rail thin in his youth he also was being forced to fight off a middle-aged paunch; the loose skin of his neck was evidence of his victories and defeats in that regard. It was said that the man was a good officer and had the respect of his soldiers, so he also was valuable to Handrick, who doubted that the cavalry would be willing to follow an outsider. Firth had never had a large cavalry and those who served under that banner were a tight-knit group.

To his left was Azchod, a Were like Handrick and the smartest of those who carried the Curse. In his previous life Azchod had been a scholar in one of the free cities, and a successful merchant as well before the Curse overwhelmed him. Of all the Weres only Azchod was physically powerful enough to possibly consider himself Handrick's equal. Thankfully he was not ambitious and could be relied upon to enforce his commander's orders among the Weres. For that reason alone he was valuable.

Directly across from Handrick sat Colonel von Tirek. The youngest of the senior Firthian officers Tirek was the commander of the Firthian Spearmen, which made up the largest element of the army. Handrick didn't like Tirek; the man was simply too difficult to control and had an annoying habit of thinking for himself. Tirek was the first to question every order given. He also had his uses, but nothing so important that Handrick wouldn't gladly replace him at the first opportunity. This very night would not be soon enough. It was important that he not kill the man outright, he couldn't afford a revolt among the troops, but Handrick planned to order the colonel to lead every battle until the man was eliminated.

To Azchod's left was the Smirek, and for him Handrick had no use whatsoever.

His title translated as 'Grand Liaison' and Handrick had been ordered to use the title whenever addressing the man by Duke Lionel himself. That was just as well, because if the man had a name it was never used. If there was ever a person Handrick despised on sight it was the Grand Liaison.

Soft and pudgy the man was so obese the flesh sat on him in folds. His numerous chins bounced when he rode and the horse that carried him was more suited to pulling a freight wagon than carrying a saddle. If that wasn't bad enough the man was a eunuch, the fact confirmed by his high tenor voice as well as Handrick's sensitive nose; he smelled like neither a man or a woman, but rather a perfumed combination that nauseated all the Weres forced to be around him. Dressed in a black robe containing enough fabric to clothe the horse he rode, the eunuch wore a great deal of jewelry including a prominent nose ring. The Grand Liaison was the agent the duke contacted to hire the Signalers and the witches treated the man like a prince. Not once had Handrick ever seen the man when he wasn't eating and the huge pack strapped on behind him was rumored to be full of nothing but food.

A Were's instinct was to kill, particularly humans and more particularly men, and to feed upon the flesh of their victims. But Handrick knew that if he ever did have the opportunity to kill the Grand Liaison it would not be to feed; he couldn't imagine taking a bite from such a one as he. Even the thought brought a foul, cloying taste to his mouth. No, Handrick had no use for the Grand Liaison; he was capable of explaining what he wanted to the witches. But to dispose of the man would deny Handrick's army the use of the Signalers as well as bringing the wrath of the sisters down on him.

"We made good time," Handrick stated. "The Signalers lived up to their claims. Are we yet concealed from magical eyes?"

If the man's appearance, existence, and mannerisms were not

offensive enough, the Grand Liaison only spoke in a high-pitched lisping sing-song. "The sisters appreciate your praise great general and wish to assure you that they have deflected all prying eyes."

"Any word from the city?" Handrick asked, pointedly looking in the Grand Liaison's eyes so he wouldn't have to address the man by his title.

The man paused a moment, cutting his eyes dramatically up and to the left as if looking at someone sitting in a tree and showing his bulging, bloodshot eyes to the Were. "The sisters have heard nothing from their sisters in the city; but neither have they heard their lives pass through the singing gate."

Handrick didn't even want to know what the fellow meant by the last part of his response; no signal had as of yet been heard from the Signalers in the city was sufficient for him.

"What report from the flankers?" he asked Colonel Barant. The cavalry commander was ready.

"The left flank reports encountering two people; a young couple that slipped from their homes, intent on meeting with one another. The man was killed and the woman tied up and delivered to the baggage train. The right flank reports nothing; the Quargs are apparently doing their jobs there."

"General Intona, what of our troops? Were all able to keep up?"

"Yes sir, no problems other than a couple of the mercenary companies leaving formation and falling behind when they stepped out of the Signaler's travel spell."

"Why did they do that?" queried Azchod. The Were's voice sounded amused.

Intona snorted his derision. "The fools were trying to pass the Firthian companies ahead of them; to beat them to the city and so as to have a better chance of finding good spoils."

The group laughed quietly, all except for the Grand Liaison who smiled broadly, he had no teeth, and forced another piece of softened jerky into his already packed mouth.

"Don't the fools realize that they'll have all the plunder they can carry when we take the city?" asked Azchod, the Were's sense of humor all but causing him to laugh out loud at the foolishness of the mercenaries. The city was said to be the home of more than eighty thousand people; some of them nobility or rich merchants. Everyone would soon be as rich as their saddlebags would allow.

"They're mercenaries," Intona said, meaning it as an insult. The others simply accepted it as the best explanation.

"Let's review our plans. Once we enter by the main gate the cavalry will..." Handrick began only to be interrupted by a high crooning sound emanating from the Grand Liaison.

"Isn't it beautiful?" he squealed, his piggish eyes staring through the branches towards the sky above Aldrigal City. The others immediately turned in their saddles to see what he meant, but found the sky as dark as before. The Signaler, however, was now trembling, her mouth open in amazement as she also stared into the sky.

"What is it?" Handrick demanded. "Grand Liaison, what do you see?"

A string of drool emerged from one corner of his mouth as the man spoke around his food. "It is a great bird; a phoenix of power clothed in red, blue and purple. It has taken flight from the great city and adorned its brightest plumage to attract us; to lure us as its mate to pursue it for the glory of the Signaler's Guild."

"What did he say?" demanded an exasperated Intona. If possible he had even less use for the Grand Liaison than did Handrick. At least the Were somewhat understood what the Signalers, and their obese representative, were capable of.

"The Signalers in the city have just communicated that they have the gates," Handrick said, studying the Grand Liaison for some sign that what he was saying was accurate. "Correct, Grand Liaison?"

Chortling, the fat man swallowed the huge mouthful of meat without bothering to wipe away what had flowed from his mouth. Any thoughts the others might have that he was clearing his mouth to be more easily understood was forgotten when the Grand Liaison shoved another fist full of dried meat in before speaking again.

"The magnificent general has spoken the truth and indeed it is so. The glorious sisters on their mission of stealth have brought forth the lamp of education to shine upon our ignorance," he half-sang.

"Get everyone on their feet," growled Handrick, cutting the fat man off before he burst completely into song. "Bring everyone up even with the tree line; weapons in their hands and ready to move."

Without another word the officers saluted and hurried to their places, shouting orders and cursing where necessary to move the soldiers to theirs. As prearranged the cavalries of Firth and Kelsten moved out beyond the trees, ready to utilize both the speed of their mounts and the magical enhancement to reach the city gates as quickly as possible. Once they were inside, the city had to fall; the guardsmen couldn't hope to stand up to them.

Handrick smelled a host of odors on the breeze; the stench of over-ripe pomegranate from the perfume on the Grand Liaison, the combined smell of fear and anticipation from the human soldiers, and the faint scent of a sleeping mok curled somewhere nearby in its deep burrow. Once he received the signal that the soldiers were in place all would be ready; the invasion would finally begin in earnest. His horse hopped eagerly from hoof to hoof, picking up the excitement of its rider as the Were watched for the waving of the flag that would come from his left. The anticipation was enormous and Handrick almost remembered what it was like to be young again.

Then it came, a single flash of white within the stygian darkness of the trees. No human could have seen it; but he had.

"Do it now," he ordered to the Grand Liaison.

His head lolling back in what Handrick hoped was a signal of acceptance and not the obese man having a long overdue stroke, the Grand Liaison hooted softly twice and then began staring directly into the back of the nearby Signaler. The woman jumped as if poked with a needle, and began waving her arms furiously before urging her horse out in front of the cavalry. Once there she kicked her mount into a canter, then to a full run as the cavalry hurried to keep up.

Handrick's lips pulled back in a snarl; it was all he could do not to allow the change to overtake him so great was his excitement. Channeling his enthusiasm into movement he spurred his horse out into the open and shouted once to gain everyone's attention.

"Move out men, it's time to put Aldrigal to the torch."

# Chapter Eleven

Burstis sat panting after his long run, his fur sweaty despite the chill air. The tree he sat beneath was an evergreen, giving him some cover from those he watched. It wouldn't do for them to see him just yet.

Humans were stupid; he'd known that for some time now and regretted ever being one himself. He had trailed a number of them for days just to discover where the refugees were fleeing to and none of them had even known he was there.

The hill he sat upon was the last before the land became more level and was largely cleared of standing timber by the stupid farmers that lived below. The refugees had fled to a town there, trusting in the ridiculous wooden palisade they hid behind to give them some sense of comfort. Perhaps it might provide some defense from marauding Quargs, they were even more stupid than were humans, but it was useless to prevent someone such as him from gaining entrance. A Were was, after all, superior to a human in every conceivable way.

His hip still hurt from the wound he had received at the hands of the one-armed boy. For one whole day he had hidden in a thicket and licked it, allowing the Quargs to pass him by along with any risk that his brother Weres might be in the area before he had changed back to his human form. Where had the whelp gotten a magical weapon? Burstis had found the little blade in the road and had taken great joy in destroying it.

And then he had picked up the boy's trail, or tried to. Burstis couldn't imagine why the boy had not changed into his Were form when fighting him but he certainly had embraced it since then. As near as he could tell the boy had remained a Were from that time on, if Burstis could trust his sense of smell.

He had tried to trail the boy, hoping he would lead him to the old woman and anyone else that may have survived the crash of the carriage. If the Quargs had them, which was very possible, his job was all but finished. However he dared not interrogate any of the humanoids for fear of Handrick finding out he was nearby. The Were general, who should be busy supervising the invasion of Aldrigal, hated Burstis and had the resources to track him down and kill him.

Then his luck had turned bad; the boy did not catch up to the old woman as Burstis had hoped. Adding further insult; he had then lost the trail of the boy. Casting about desperately he had finally stumbled across the scent of other humans, whole groups of them, fleeing the Quargs and had followed them here. If they came here any survivors from his own attack might have as well. There certainly wasn't anything else around here for them to flee to.

But now Burstis had a decision to make. When darkness came he could circle the town at his leisure and test for the now familiar scent of Gran if she had left the area. If she had entered the town from any direction, he should be able to detect her assuming she had entered on her own feet. If she had ridden or been carried, his odds of detecting her were much less. He had no hope of scenting her from outside the town, even if the wind was right; there were simply too many odors contained within the walls for that. If his circle of the town did not turn up her scent, then he would have to decide what to do next; it was possible that the old hag was already in some Quarg stewpot. Therein lay his decision. How to be certain?

The breeze changed, bringing the scent of a wolf pack to Burstis' sensitive nose. They might be feral, but they could also be some of the half-tamed beasts enthralled by the Quargs. That a band of the humanoids might be approaching made sense; the human refugees below were certainly running from something but Burstis knew that this area was somewhat south of Firth's invasion plans. Quargs were not to be trusted, however, and might well have strayed from their duties.

At least his next tasks were clear; search the area for Quargs today and the lowlands for signs of Gran tonight. By morning he may be in the walled town; the pitifully stupid humans couldn't hope to keep him out.

# Chapter Twelve

The man named Tomo was easy to find, he was lingering over the still-unconscious woodsman soothing the man's brow with a wet rag. Once he had been identified Jamus approached him.

"I didn't know he was feverish," Jamus said. The man named Tomo looked up before responding.

"He's not, but Gran told me to do this, so that's what I'm doing," Tomo replied.

Jamus chuckled. "It's just easier to do what Gran says, right?"

Tomo smiled in return. "You must have met her."

The two men introduced themselves and shook hands. Looking around the room Jamus found it largely empty save for empty cots. Only two were occupied; the one with the woodsman and another nearby that held a youth of about fifteen wearing a set of splints on one leg.

"How is your patient doing?"

Tomo rinsed his rag again, though it did little or no good as both cloth and water were filthy. "Better; he awoke last evening and ate three-quarters of a hog, if the ladies that were caring for him are to be believed. Gran gave him something to make him sleep, claiming that he needed that more than anything else now. His wound remains clear."

"That is wonderful news. The fellow contributed greatly to saving our lives," Jamus said then wondered aloud. "Where is Gran?"

"She's in the kitchens, through that door," Tomo pointed. "She's sitting in a chair where she can supervise everything that's going on. Setting that boy's broken leg took all her strength."

Jamus was stunned. "Gran set the boy's leg? She's been unconscious for days, and has a broken leg herself! I thought she was dying!"

Tomo laughed loud and long. "She's tough, our Gran. Truth be told, I'm amazed too. I saw what her head looked like as the healers were bandaging it. I doubt that I could have survived the same wound."

Jamus slumped onto the next cot, shaking his head in wonder. "I have to agree. I cleaned that wound more than once on the trail, and it looked bad, really bad."

"Well if it's any consolation to you, Gran has been surprising people longer than both of us have been alive... combined."

"I'll take your word for it. I haven't known her that long. What about you?"

"All my life," Tomo said, returning to washing the woodsman's forehead. "She delivered me and my brothers. My mom too, it's said, but I know better than to ask." Tomo winked conspiratorially towards Jamus. "Gran doesn't like to discuss her age."

Dropping the cloth into the grimy water, Tomo joined Jamus on the cot.

"So how did you and Gran meet?"

Jamus saw no reason to withhold the information so he told Tomo about meeting Gran in Aldrigal City and agreeing to give her a ride to Skallist. The attack on the road he glossed over somewhat; not revealing the presence of any Weres but giving most of the credit for their downfall to the Quargs.

"Sounds like a pretty rough ride," grunted Tomo. "Where did you pick up this guy? Surely he wasn't serving you as a coachman."

"No, I'd never seen him before he came out of the forest and jumped on my carriage. He and another man, a much younger man, did all they could to save us."

Tomo tried not to look too interested but it was plainly obvious to the viscount. "And what did Gran say about them?"

"Not much, but she plainly knew them. The boy at least she seemed to know very well. She even told him that she loved him; which means she thought that she was dying. That was right before the carriage flipped over."

Nodding slowly to himself Tomo thought long before speaking again. "Did she happen to mention his name?"

Jamus was becoming a little wary at this point; Tomo was hiding something and Gran had been running from someone. Tomo remained wary as he was afraid to reveal something that Gran didn't want him to.

"No, not that I recall. He knew her name, called her 'Gran' quite plainly. I was somewhat disoriented at the time; my wife was dying in my arms."

"Ah, I'm sorry to hear that My Lord. It's hard to lose a loved one."

Jamus choked up and Tomo gave a moment to collect himself. Eventually he regained control and smiled. "My Lord? I didn't say anything about being a noble. How did you know?"

"It's pretty obvious, My Lord. Your speech, your mannerisms, you don't talk like a peasant."

"I'll try to do better. Let's keep this our secret for now, Tomo. Gran knows but no one else. I get the feeling that the nobility isn't well liked around here."

Tomo agreed to his request and they spent a few moments discussing inconsequential matters; each feeling the other out. Finally

Jamus decided to probe lightly for information about the other man.

"And what of you, Tomo? What brings you here?"

"Fleeing for my life, same as everyone else," Tomo laughed. "It was providence, or luck, or a combination of the two that I managed to get my family out. I had been at Spicer, answering questions from the authorities who were looking for Gran. They've kept me on a tight leash since she left. Being an acquaintance of a known fugitive can get to be a nuisance at times. I was on my way home when I saw Quargs in the forest, and they were acting strangely."

"Strange in what way? I would think everything about Quargs would be strange."

"That's well said, because Quargs are peculiar to say the least. They don't think like we do, and that's a fact. But Quargs normally only come to the lowlands to raid, and they don't bother much with stealth when they do. By their way of thinking it's to their advantage for their enemies to know they're coming, providing they have overwhelming force, hoping that they'll run away and leave their valuables behind for easy looting. Not a lot of warning, but a few minutes at least. These Quargs were being almighty careful to be quiet, which means they were acting as a screen."

"A screen?"

"Yes, they were trying to quietly take out anyone they came across so that no word would escape to warn others. I recognized it for what it was; perhaps not an invasion but certainly an attack with enough warriors to wipe out my little village. I hid inside a hollow tree until I caught a glimpse of what the Quargs were screening, and then I hightailed it for home, gathered up the family, and got out of the area."

"Human Cavalry, I'm told."

"Yep, big and bold as brass and moving fast. They was like the barbarians in that story 'The Jackdog and the Conquering Horde," do you remember that one?"

"I believe so; the Jackdog encountered a horde of rampaging barbarians who prided themselves on their swift movement. Unfortunately for them they moved so fast they forgot to defend their backsides and so were tricked by the Jackdog with their own dust cloud into thinking that a bigger army was coming up behind them."

"That's the one. These men weren't traveling, they weren't marching, they were in an all-fired big hurry to be somewhere. That meant they weren't worried about being seen or had taken steps to ensure that they couldn't be seen. In our area there are only a few small villages; most anyone living outside them was killed in the Were raid a year or so back, so to me that meant that the villages were being destroyed as they went. Since my home was in their path, I did what I could to warn everyone. A few families came with me and some went other directions."

"You outran cavalry? Must be pretty swift on your feet."

"Nah, I just know all the short cuts. You don't travel far in any one direction in those hills when riding horses; you have to do a lot of going around. While they were attacking one village, I cut over to Cobble and got my folks."

"Not really cavalry country?"

"Not by a long shot."

"Makes sense in a way I suppose; if you're going to invade, travel through an area that's sparsely population so no one knows you're coming."

"Right enough; but it still doesn't make a lot of sense to me; I've lived in that area for a few years now and know it pretty well. I just can't figure out where they came from. If they came from the opposite direction they were going towards, they were coming out of the Kenebruks. No one crosses those, not this time of year at least, and never on horseback."

"Are they that rugged? I always traveled around, of course, but I've heard people say they're the tallest mountains in the world."

"I don't know about that, but they're awfully rugged. The only way I can see to get a horse over those mountains is to cut him up and pack the pieces on your back; because you're going to be doing a lot of vertical climbing. Even if you make it, the horse won't be in much of a shape to help you."

They shared a chuckle. "I suppose not. So the invaders came from the north or the south then, following along the mountains before cutting over?"

"I suppose, but that don't make much sense either. Since the Were War there just aren't any other kingdoms in a position to invade Aldrigal; other than Skallist and those weren't elves on those horses."

Jamus shrugged. "Did you catch a glimpse of any heraldry? A shield or banner?"

Tomo gave the matter some thought as he rested his chin on his fist and rocked gently back and forth. Finally he replied, "There was one; it was blue, had a golden bird-looking thing on it with a crooked line," he made a motion in the air to describe it, "and two wheat sheaves above that, I think. Sorry; I only got a quick glimpse."

Now it was Jamus' turn to think. The heraldry Tomo described had a vaguely familiar feel about it but he couldn't quite think of anyone who carried it. Heraldry was supposed to be unique for each individual but kingdoms rarely shared this information between themselves and duels between nobles with similar symbols were commonplace. Some kings chose a primary color and decreed that all those who served them must use that color in their own arms, but blue was very popular. Eventually Jamus had to admit that he was blank.

"Nothing! But perhaps something will come to me later; I've

traveled a great deal and have known many who use the hawk, phoenix, eagle, griffon, etc on their personal arms. My own family uses the cockerel, but I promise they are not involved in any current invasions."

"What is your nation of origin sir, if I may be so bold."

"I am from Rotgaren, Tomo. On the eastern coast. Very old kingdom, and very peaceful. No one bothers us much anymore."

"I've heard of it. A really large navy, right?"

"True, many Rotgarens have taken to the sea, and our navy is our power both in war and trade."

Tomo nodded silently, finding nothing to comment on in the nobleman's words. He'd never seen the ocean, nor a boat larger than a river barge, so had no experiences to draw a comparison to.

"Oh, and I nearly forgot," Tomo then added. "The really odd thing about where I saw the Quargs, at least at the time, was where they were."

"What do you mean?"

"Well there are certain areas in any forest you learn to avoid. In some places there are bears, or even griffons as you mentioned before, and you learn to stay out of their hunting grounds as much as possible. Same for the Quargs; you learn where they go and you just don't go there. It's the same for the Quargs themselves; they generally avoid certain areas just out of plain good common sense."

"But not this time?"

"No sir. There's one stretch of forest no body that knows better goes into, because of this legend said to live there. A man who's part demon, and kills anyone that trespasses on his land. The Quargs call him the Keon-din, and the nobles call him a thief and worst; there are wanted posters for him all along the main roads. The Quargs won't usually enter his hunting grounds, and where I saw them they must have passed directly through there."

Suddenly Jamus understood. "You mean this fellow don't you," he said, pointing to the woodsman on the cot.

"Yes I do, My Lord," stated Tomo, looking Jamus in the eye for the first time.

"Friend of yours, I take it?"

"In a manner of speaking, yes. When I was a boy he was just enough older than me to be somewhat of a hero of mine; I followed him everywhere. He taught me a lot about the wilderness, and how to survive there. Next to Gran and my own family I don't think that there's anyone in the world I care for more than this man."

"Is revealing this putting you in any sort of danger?"

"Probably not; I'm not wanted and had nothing to do with anything that made him wanted; most people have long ago separated the man he was from the man he is, if you know what I mean. Most folks believe that the man I knew is dead; but I felt like I needed to say something to you about him, because those scars make him mighty noticeable."

Jamus glanced at the thick mass of scars on the woodsman's neck. They were horrible and should have killed the man when he got them.

Tomo continued. "I figure that since you're with Gran that you probably aren't the type to try anything but I just wanted you to know; if you try to turn him in, or let anyone else in on his identity, I'll take it personally."

"Personally?"

"Yes, My Lord, I'll kill you deader than a stone."

Jamus didn't bother to tell Tomo that that secret may already be out.

# Chapter Thirteen

Burstis dropped to his belly and allowed his tongue to hang, seeking to cool his wolf form. Despite the cold of the night he was hot from his circle of the village; it had taken him hours to accomplish. Daylight was no more than an hour away now and even his Were strength was being taxed.

Naturally he had found no scent of the woman; surely the Quargs had already finished her. However Burstis knew not to take any chances when serving the Duke of Firth. Kill the woman he had been told, along with the one-armed Were boy, and that he would do if possible.

Behind him stood a large house, abandoned he knew. The place was built like a fortress but not even the iron-banded door could resist his strength. He had spent the previous day there resting in his man-form in case anyone happened by. It was like many he had found in the area; large, defensible, and abandoned.

Burstis forced himself into the change. If a human was found here, even a nude man, it would cause less of a problem than would a wolf but he still didn't enjoy the process. The pain was incredible; much worse than changing from human to Were. Burstis had begun to believe that was an element of his distaste for his human form; were it not for the occasional advantages he would almost rather remain a wolf. At the last moment he changed his mind and chose the half-wolf half-man form.

The change complete he rose to his feet and made his way up the steps and into the house. It was cold, bitterly cold, and his human form would have suffered. In this form he still had his fur and the ability to build a fire with his hands. The bottom floor was one large room; another commonality to the homes he had explored, with a large fireplace in the center. His hands were not nimble in this form, but a quantity of flammable oil was available along with a large supply of firewood and smaller sticks as well. In no time Burstis had a fire going and then completed the change to human form.

It was still cold. Burstis stood as closely to the fire as he could and shivered for a time before the warmth took effect. Once he felt under control he put on the clothing he'd left there and wrapped himself in a blanket.

The clothing had come from the house as well; he'd taken them from a wardrobe upstairs and were likely their previous owner's second-best. The boots were a little large for him and were worn dangerously thin on the bottom. Why the farmer had even kept them Burstis had no idea, but he was glad for even their minimal protection from the icy cold floor.

Having fed well on a stray sheep encountered on his journey, Burstis was not hungry but drank deeply from a bucket of water before filling a copper pot with the same. Then he curled up before the fire and napped there until the sun was up.

Stretching after sleeping on the hard floor, Burstis took the time to wash himself in the pot before scattering the firewood and dumping the remaining water on the coals to reduce any smoke. Some farmer might get angry if he saw smoke coming from his chimney and Burstis didn't want to start trouble just yet. Next he gathered up a jacket and a cloak he had harvested and put them all on before stepping outside. A light dusting of snow was on the ground now and he was unused to the chill air after spending so many days in wolf form recently. The house he had chosen was one of the closer structures to the village so the walk wouldn't be too extreme.

Having never been a farmer Burstis was unsure as to what the various smaller outbuildings and tools he saw were for but he didn't waste time trying to figure any of it out. He chose an odd-looking tool with a handle nearly as tall as himself topped by a curved wooden blade longer than his arm from its rack to carry with him. With the residents all hiding in the village word about the Quargs was obviously about and a man walking around unarmed would look suspicious. Being that he was also carrying a farm implement seemed to somehow complete his disguise.

Using the scythe as a walking staff, Burstis set out along the road towards the village. He was approaching the gates almost directly on, so he would be seen pretty quickly. A band of riders, probably scouts out looking for the approaching Quarg horde, left the gate as he was approaching but they only waved to him before riding on.

Two nights before Burstis had inspected the village and their odd-looking walls. The logs had been coated in some mixture that would not allow even his Curse-powered claws to find a hold so climbing them was impractical if not impossible. So he had decided to just walk in.

"Hello the walls," Burstis yelled when he felt that he was close enough. A pair of heads were watching him from atop the gate but they didn't yell back, one merely motioning him on. Once he had crossed half the distance a tall, thin woman carrying a bow stepped from the still open gates and watched him approach; an arrow ready but not pointed at him. After he approached a little more she visibly relaxed and returned the arrow to her quiver.

"He's no Quarg, Kleg. Not a 'breed neither," she yelled, tilting her head back to look up at the top of the gate. Returning her gaze to Burstis she asked, "Who are you stranger? What's your business in Vicksville?"

Burstis gave the woman his most disarming smile; negotiation was what he was best at and had been his life's ambition before the Curse. "Dear lady I am but a simple traveler who lost his way fleeing the Quargs. I was hoping to find protection behind these impressive walls."

She grunted, not showing any signs that she was taken by his charms. "That's not up to me, stranger, but I doubt they'll turn you away. I'll take you to see the mayor."

Beyond the gates, which were closed behind them after they entered, Burstis found a small village of several hundred people that was now seemed choked with more than twice what it was designed to hold. The press of the crowds was almost more than his enhanced sense of smell could stand so thick was the miasma of unwashed bodies, wood smoke, and well used outhouses.

Cook fires were scattered here and there and people were sleeping wherever they could find a place they wouldn't be trampled on. Some of the side streets were dead ends and they had been fenced off to contain animals. Wagons of freshly cut hay were being unloaded into barns, filling up every space to maximize the quantity the buildings could hold. These people were preparing for a siege and, Burstis decided, they were well rehearsed in the task.

"Mayor Lauder should be at the inn, I'll take you there," his guide said at one point. "If he's not there, someone should know where he is."

Burstis tried to thank the woman, even dropped some subtle compliments to gauge her response but received little reaction. He had begun to think he had lost his touch when they reached their destination.

The woman walked up to a handsome young man standing near the door of the inn and gathered him into a passionate embrace. The two spoke quietly for a moment as Burstis waited. Finally the man left and the woman turned back to him.

"Sorry, my husband and I were only married a few days ago; preparing for the siege interrupted our festivities. Mayor Lauder is inside; upstairs and to the end of the hall, last door on the right." She stepped back and pointed to window above and to their left. "That room there. Tell him your story and he'll tell whether or not you can stay. He won't turn you down."

"Thank you, my lady," Burstis said, offering her a partial bow.

Stepping through the door brought Burstis into a large common room, once again taking up the entire bottom floor of the building.

"Have these people never heard of walls or privacy?" Burstis grouched.

His meeting with Lauder went quickly; the man had more details to deal with then he could keep up with and so accepted Burstis' explanations almost without question. The man was certainly no farmer and the clothes he wore didn't even fit him, but after the mayor shared a story of one refugee apparently having been found wearing nothing but a silken loincloth he wasn't even suspicious.

"You'll have to find a place to stay; all the inns are full and the common rooms as well. All the citizens have been told to take in anyone they can, and most have complied. Being a stranger I wouldn't expect anything in that regard. The barns are all full of hay, so those aren't an option, but you might find a place in the street or on top of someone's roof if you don't mind freezing to death."

"Uh, thanks I guess," Burstis said sarcastically. Lauder didn't even notice. "Any chance I could buy some supplies, maybe take my chances outrunning the Quargs? Has anyone even seen any Quargs around here?"

"To the north, yes," Lauder said, looking through a stack of parchments. "Refugees from there have seen them, and our outermost scouts have seen signs of their passage. We don't know that they're coming here, but we don't know that they're not either."

"You've had a lot of refugees?"

"Yes, quite a few. Most were from villages that used to be to our north and west, but they're all gone now. Some were from travelers from the main road, such as yourself."

"Ah, well then perhaps you can help me. I lost track of some of my companions from the road, they were moving this direction the last I knew but we were separated."

"I doubt it, friend, we've got a lot of strangers here. You're welcome to look around the village; there's not that many people here that you couldn't see them all in a day."

"Perhaps if I described them for you; they're somewhat memorable."

Lauder was growing frustrated. "I need somewhere to store more grain due in from the farms and have a family of five sleeping in my privy. On top of that I possibly have a horde of Quarg on their way here and I have to defend this entire town with around three hundred able but untrained bodies. I do not have time for this, sir!"

I beg your pardon, mayor, but this is my family we're talking about," Burstis shouted, tears flowing freely down his face. Acting was another skill he was adept in. "It will take but a moment, and then I will go search the village if you cannot remember, please! I have to start somewhere; you meet everyone that comes here."

Lauder calmed himself with an effort and threw his parchments onto the bed beside him. "Fine, describe them for me."

Burstis took a moment to feign fear before beginning. He decided to begin with the person he remembered best from the carriage. "One was a boy with his right hand missing below the elbow."

"Arm missing? Certainly, I've seen a couple of those, but not a youth. Not that I can remember anyway, I'm sorry."

That's fine, it may very well be that they were separated," Burstis replied, deciding to skip the two men from the carriage as the only one he had a good look was the pampered little noble and he was very average in appearance. Of the other man he only remembered arrows striking him with surprising power.

"The other was a woman; an older woman. She's somewhat stooped with age, her hair is very gray," he began, giving a good description of Gran and the clothes she had been wearing at the carriage. Not having any clue as to her personality he resorted to his own imagination to supply that.

"Wonderful old lady, loved by everyone. As sweet an old grandmother as you'll ever meet," he finished.

Lauder's interest died immediately. Laughing he replied, "Oh, for a moment there I thought you were talking about Gran."

# Chapter Fourteen

Tomo groaned as he dropped the empty bucket. Behind him the hogs he had just slopped were grunting excitedly as they fed on the scraps. Grabbing his lower back he worked to ease the pain; he wasn't used to such labor. Had it really only been a week?

Gran was healthier every day and had become the tyrant in charge of caring for the wounded in short order. Women who had served the village for generations quickly came to heal under her and no one seemed to find it odd that they obeyed her every command. It certainly didn't take long for them all to realize that the old woman knew more than all of them combined about caring for the sick and wounded.

Kicking the bucket over to where the second one already lay, Tomo used one bend-over to retrieve both, groaning again as he straightened.

"I can't take much more of this," he told himself. He'd once volunteered to track a wounded bear for Lord Ferule to avoid work far less strenuous than what the citizens of Vicksville had forced upon him. He wasn't made for city life. Once he had his buckets he waited for the one person in the village more miserable than himself.

"My palms are bleeding," Jamus whined, the viscount had maintained his pose as a commoner at Gran's urging; the citizens of Freeman's Green were even less fond of the nobility than he had originally feared. Unfortunately this required them to work for their meals if they couldn't pay for them, and Jamus' small stash of coins was too precious to part with just yet; or so Gran maintained. Jamus was almost ready to sign away his birthright for a decent meal and a night on a soft mattress.

"Let me see," demanded Tomo, who dropped his buckets in order to inspect the other man's hands. They were indeed bleeding and showed cuts all over the palms and lower fingers.

"You have the softest hands I've ever seen," Tomo said. "Just keep the cuts clean like Gran said and eventually you'll have some nice calluses."

"She wants me to use soap made from ashes! That stuff burns worse than the cuts do themselves," Jamus stated, his face as close to a pout as Tomo had ever seen from a grown man.

"It's called lye soap, and Gran says that stinging is what keeps the cuts clean."

"I don't care what it's called; I was not made for this kind of work."

"You and me both, brother," Tomo sighed. "Come on, we'd better head back. It'll be time for the noon meal soon and we've drug this out as long as we dare."

Gathering up their buckets they set out for the town hall building, using short cuts learned the hard way to get past the press of people. Lauder had been forced to ask some of the refugees if they would mind pitching tents outside the walls, and he had had far more volunteers than he had expected. Tomo had been one but his wife had vetoed the offer. He saw no reason to dwell within all this humanity until the Quargs were close, and so far there had not been any seen in the area of Freedom's Green.

The two crossed a corral full of cattle and then stepped over the cook fire of a family sheltered in the next alley. This brought them out onto a street one over from where they needed to be. Looking to their right they saw that the main thoroughfare, as Jamus had sardonically named the main street that ran the length of Vicksville, remained as crowded as ever so they climbed over a board fence and cut through a butcher's shop to reach their street. Working their way across the road took some time between the crowds and the sheep, but finally they reached their destination.

"I figured the hogs had made a meal out of you," groused Gran, who was waiting for them as they came through the door. Jamus would have said that she 'pounced' upon them even with the splint on her leg.

"Sorry Gran, it's impossible to get anywhere fast through all those people."

Gran sniffed. "Drunks and lay-abouts all, like as not. What they need is someone to show them the work that needs to be done and then see that they do it, that's all."

Sitting back on her stool Gran surveyed her little empire; the makeshift hospital now had three patients counting the woodsman and the boy with the broken leg. A girl of twelve had fallen and hit her head on a wagon wheel and promptly been placed in the female section of the hospital, that is to say the far corner from the men. Behind Gran the kitchen was working at full capacity to provide simple meals for the refugees. A copper coin a day bought you three filling, if somewhat tasteless and boring, meals and with the way prices were soaring it was barely enough to keep the larders full.

"How is our friend doing?" Jamus asked, pointing towards the woodsman. The man was sitting up and a woman was busily spooning something from a bowl into him. The man didn't seem overly excited by the meal but was obediently taking it in.

Smiling Gran replied, "Very well. He'll be fit to travel in a week or so, like as not. Sooner perhaps, the boy is strong as a bull."

Tomo took a tentative sniff. "Porridge again, Gran?"

Gran immediately took offense. "Yes its porridge, and there's nothing better for a body than a good bowl of porridge! Lay-abouts and ne'er-do-wells probably won't appreciate it, but it's wholesome and fit enough for a king."

"Yes Gran," the two men intoned. There was no use complaining; the meals were simple by need not choice. Lauder was planning for the worst.

"Did you still want to talk to us at the noon meal, Gran?" asked Jamus.

Gran harrumphed. "I said so didn't I? As soon as you have your porridge, meet me over there," she said, pointing towards a table near the fireplace. Both men nodded and left quickly before Gran realized that she hadn't yet given them anything else to do.

Tomo's timing remained good and they only waited a few moments before the bell was rung to announce that the noon meal was ready. Naturally they were first in line; Jamus appreciated those traits in Tomo.

Taking their bowls the two sat as near to the fire as they could and shared a forlorn look before taking that first bite. It wasn't that the porridge tasted bad, or even that it tasted worse than anyone else's porridge, but for some reason it remained the only food that Gran couldn't seem to make more appetizing. In fact, it was so bland as to be tasteless.

"I love porridge with honey," Tomo said, taking his first bite.

Jamus perked up noticeably at his words. "You have honey in yours?"

"No," Tomo replied. "I just like it when I do."

Even though they weren't enamored with their meal both men lingered over it as long as possible, agreeing that there was no need to rush through to whatever Gran had planned for them. As usual Gran didn't join them until everyone needing a meal had passed through the line, taking her bowl last before joining the men by the fire, balancing it easily despite her crutch.

"Let's move over there, she said, leading the way to a cot in one corner. No one else sat close by as it was the furthest spot from the fire and so the coldest corner in the room. Pulling her shawl tighter over her shoulders, Gran motioned for the men to sit on the cot across from her.

Gran shoveled her porridge down in record time and sat the bowl between her feet before speaking.

"I need to leave."

Too stunned to reply the men didn't immediately respond.

"You can't leave, Gran," stammered Jamus. "What about your leg?"

"The Quargs could be here any day," blurted Tomo.

"I know, I've heard the stories," Gran quipped, almost smiling. "And I am very much aware of the pain in my leg but unfortunately I have things I have to do. Now."

"Have you forgotten the Were that attacked us?" asked Jamus. "He called you by name! There's no reason to think that he's not still after you. I heard wolves howling every night on the way here; it could have been him."

"And probably was, like as not," responded Gran. "But there's another Were out there that I care about; he needs me and I have to help him. It's my fault he's..." Gran sputtered, tears welling in her eyes. "He's gone wild and has no hope of helping himself. I'm responsible for it."

"Responsible how?" demanded Jamus. "You didn't Curse him."

"I'm responsible, and if you'll bear with me I'll tell you how."

Tomo sat up a little straighter. "Gran are you sure you want to..."

"Yes," she spat, producing a switch from somewhere and holding it threateningly. "I think I know when I want to tell something and who I want to tell it too! And don't be so sure you know everything I'm going to say, Tomo, because there's more to this story."

Looking like a scolded child the woodsman sat back on the cot looking sheepish. Gran's face softened along with her voice as she put the switch away.

"I'll begin with the part that Jamus doesn't know. More than a year ago a Were led a bunch of wolves into some attacks in the area Tomo and I lived in. In the end he killed everyone in one village and then attacked ours. My son died, and my grandson lost an arm."

Jamus was surprised again and looked it; he remembered the one-armed young man at the carriage.

"And yes, he gained the Curse because of it. I killed the Were, but lost my family. And I was responsible because Albrim, my grandson, lost his arm trying to save me."

"That's not true Gran, he was protecting his father, his village, just like we all were," Tomo protested.

The switch again appeared like magic. "Don't you know better than to interrupt your elders?"

"Sorry Gran."

"Like I said, I was responsible," she restated, glaring at Tomo as if daring him to speak again. "I did what I could for Albrim; I saw him through the loss of his arm and treated him as best I could for the hydrophobee he also got from the Were, then I faked his death and sent him away to where he would be cared for, in the woods, with someone I trusted."

Tomo almost spoke again but held his tongue just in time.

"While Albrim was in hiding with him," she pointed her chin towards the sleeping woodsman across the room, "his Curse was managed. In other words he was chained up like an animal whenever the moons were full or close to it. Eventually many of those with the

Curse can learn to control their changes, and even maintain their intelligence and reason whenever they are in their other form. Unfortunately, because Albrim also had the hydrophobee, his chances of doing so were greatly reduced, so I arranged for another friend of mine to make something to help him."

Looking directly at Tomo she continued. "Yes, this is the part you don't know. So this other friend built a magical device that not only controlled the Curse, it forced it into dormancy so long as the device was worn. Albrim was still Cursed, but he could not change into wolf form no matter what. There were risks, of course; once he wore the device for more than a few weeks he could never learn to control his changes; not that he had much of a chance anyway with the disease on top of the Curse. My hope was that he could live a more normal life and perhaps survive long enough for me to think of something else; another way to help him."

"Did it work?" Tomo asked, his voice soft though he showed no fear of Gran's switch this time.

"Yes, apparently it was a great success. He was fully capable of living a normal life, so long as no one who knew he was bitten ever saw him. He couldn't ever come back home, he'd never have children," she choked up at that but took a deep breath and continued. "At least not for certain, but he would have a chance at life. And I took that away from him."

"How Gran?" asked Jamus. His voice as soft as Tomo's had been; it was difficult to see her so sad, so vulnerable. For the first time he found himself caring about this old woman and her feelings.

"How they came to be on that road when your carriage was attacked, I'll never know. But there he was and the Quargs were coming down on us and that Were had already killed your wife and your driver..." she said, openly, though quietly, sobbing now. "And all I could think about was that Albrim too, was about to die. No one could survive the Quargs and the wolves... except a Were..." her words trailed off as her hands covered her face and her sobs shook her shoulders.

Unsure how to act the two men glanced at one another and then fixed their gazes on the floor as Gran cried. If it had been anyone else they might have known how to react but not Gran. She was the strongest person either had ever known.

Faster than either expected, Gran pulled herself together and picked up her tale. "I did the only thing I could think of. To save Albrim's life I pulled the band, the magical device, from his arm. In the end it saved us," she pointed to Jamus and then herself, "otherwise the Quargs would have butchered us where we lay after the carriage overturned."

"I don't understand Gran, you took the device off him that kept him from becoming a Were, and that made him become one?"

"Yes. When I removed it Albrim changed into a Were. He's mindless as well, with no human thoughts or memories of who he was or what he could be. All Weres are like that when they are first Cursed, when they are in their other form, but my grandson has no chance now to ever advance beyond it. He can never change back to himself." She sighed. "To save his life I doomed him to spend it as a mindless beast."

# Chapter Fifteen

Darkness this pure was rare but the elements had conspired on his behalf, or against him depending on how he looked at it, on this night. He had counted on his enhanced vision, a gift of the Curse, to allow him to see when the humans could not but the old saying kept passing through Burstis' mind: 'Be sure to temper your dreams'.

Jacet had been half full this night, the larger moon plodding its slow path across the sky had risen during the day and was below the horizon before midnight. Nyret was the merest sliver and had been abroad all that day; the smaller moon would not make another appearance until just before dawn. Not even the stars were out; the thick overcast that had hung over Vicksville for days was overburdened with snow and easily sealed the village from their light. So thorough was the darkness that Lauder had ordered bonfires built outside the gates and at various points around the wall, to give the watchers above some warning of approaching enemies as well as blinding their foes to the actions of those above. The fires did nothing to illuminate the streets of the town, providing only a soft red glow that outlined the tops of the walls, and so Burstis found himself in the precarious position of not being able to see better than his prey. He didn't like the feeling.

Traveling the streets was no less crowded at night than during the day, probably more so with everyone prostrate on the ground, and Burstis was forced to walk down the main street to use the coals from the cook fires of the sleeping refugees as guides to light his way. Even then he occasionally stepped on someone, or tripped over them, and was in a foul mood before he had covered half the distance.

Three days he had spent in the stench of the unwashed humans; three days spent in the hovel of an elderly woman he had murdered his first night in town. She had no family close by, he had learned, and so she became his prey not for food, but simply for a place to stay out of sight. If Gran saw him she might very well flee and he'd have to track her down all over again.

Burstis had spent his time wisely and scouted out the village on nights when his improved vision allowed him free movement. He had even dared to take his wolf form and leap from rooftop to rooftop just to observe the building Gran was staying in. It was some type of temple, Burstis had learned, and also a meeting place of sorts. Now it was a hospital and somehow Gran had advanced from patient to being in control of it.

His last victim had had a small stack of hoarded coins he'd found when he dug up the floor of her home to hide her body. A few silver coins was all, but it was enough for Burstis to buy information from drunken locals about his true prey, and allowed him to learn quite a bit about Gran without exposing himself prematurely.

For one thing she wasn't alone. The pampered dandy from the carriage had also survived and followed her here, but Burstis certainly didn't consider the man a threat. No one in the village had any higher opinion of the noble than Burstis did, and rumors were rampant about the man. Most suspected his noble bloodlines and his lack of skill in any mundane task, along with his unceasing whining, made him both useless and distasteful to the hard working farmers.

What was truly surprising to Burstis was the presence of the larger man, the woodsman, who had stung him with the arrows back at the carriage. The man had been powerful enough to drive his arrows with such force that, despite the missiles inability to penetrate his Cursed hide, Burstis had actually felt the pain of their impact. He had believed that the woodsman had died, having smelled the man's blood on the carriage.

In truth Burstis was surprised to find any of them here, much less alive. Having found the body of the elf in the forest he suspected that the noble, if he survived and had not abandoned the wounded Gran, would have followed the road to the nearest habitation. Gran herself had been hurt and surely couldn't have walked on her own. Of the one-armed Were boy Burstis had seen no sign or smelled any scent, so he was either not here or well hid. With everyone wounded save the boy and the noble, who was far too soft to have transported the others through the forest, it only made sense to Burstis that the boy was somewhere about; either hiding in the town or nearby.

It was the only scenario that made sense; the boy had Were blood and so should have been able to convince the Quargs to leave him alone one way or another. There had been a lot of dead Quargs back on the road, and since they had no way of harming a Were would have been easy kills for someone with the Curse. Only the boy with his Were strength could have brought the others so far so fast. The uncertainty of this made Burstis cautious; otherwise he would have killed Gran the first night in Vicksville and then jumped from the top of the wall to escape. The possible presence of another Were, even a one armed boy that Burstis had neither seen nor scented, had convinced him to take it a little slower than he would have liked. So tonight he was going to try a different tact.

Finally reaching the alley, Burstis stepped over a last sleeping man and squatted down next to a large barrel from which two pairs of feet emerged. The coals of a fire were faintly glowing before the barrel and

Burstis took a moment to blow on them and bring up a fitful flare of light to see by.

Snow was falling now, thick and slow, and the tops of the two men's feet were already covered with a small lump of the stuff. Sensing no movement from the pair Burstis nudged the nearest leg, then nudged it again more firmly when he received no response. One set of snoring coming from the barrel stopped.

"Who is it?" asked a sleepy voice, the man cautiously stretching his legs out until one ankle popped loudly.

"You know who it is," Burstis replied, easing back to give the man room to emerge.

The man did so, digging his heels into the frozen mud for purchase enough to pull his body downward. Both sets of snoring stopped as he did, the two men emitting muffled curses as they tried to move about in the confined space. The barrel was large but not quite wide enough for the man to sit up fully, so he crawled out to the very edge before he tried and ended up sitting on the edge of the barrel.

"You got the money?" he asked, the tone in his voice hinting that the sleepiness of the moment before might well have been faked.

Beside the speaker his companion emerged from the barrel as well, a crossbow cocked and not quite pointing at Burstis. Brothers, Burstis assumed but hadn't bothered to confirm; he really didn't care.

"I do," Burstis whispered, placing three silver bits on the man's thigh. Life was cheap; Burstis knew that as well as anyone, but even he was amazed at just how cheap these men had bartered away the life of someone they didn't even know.

"When?" the second man whispered, patting his crossbow meaningfully. They couldn't see Burstis even half as well as he could see them, but the motion was obvious to the Were. They couldn't speak openly about murder, there were too many people around, so such hints and innuendos were necessary.

"Tonight. Now if possible," he replied, reaching he tapped the coins with a finger. "Half now, the rest upon completion."

"What's that mean?" demanded the first man, almost forgetting to keep his voice down.

"It means when the job is finished," explained his brother softly, patting his arm. "It'll be taken care of, stranger."

"It had best be," stated Burstis. "Because I am not a man that you should ever cross, and I will be here until you have completed your task."

"You'd better be, friend, because you owe us the other half of our pay," stated the second man, again patting his crossbow. Burstis almost smiled. Imagine gutter filth like this threatening a Were.

With nothing more to say Burstis stood and moved out of the alley. He had no intentions of leaving Vicksville until he was certain that the two men had accomplished what they were paid for; not until Gran was dead.

# Chapter Sixteen

Jamus awoke in the darkness, aware that something had disturbed him but not sure exactly what. He had been dreaming of eating; a whole roasted hog, complete with an apple in its mouth, along with a number of his other favorite foods sat upon a long table. His wife had been there and he had been resting on a silken divan with plentiful servants standing by to feed him any morsel he cast his gaze upon. Then he was awake.

It was too dark to be morning already, even here in this unwholesome backwater where cooks incapable of creating even one tasty dish between them arose long before sunrise to prepare the morning meal. Unable to see in the dim glow of the banked coals Jamus lay as still as possible and listened intently.

Even though he didn't see it that way himself Jamus was fortunate to be able to sleep in the hospital. So long as the bunks were unused by the injured Gran had allowed a lucky few to sleep in them and he had lain claim to the one nearest the woodsman, after Gran refused to let him have the one nearest the fire and directed him here.

Jamus heard nothing out of the ordinary; there must be at least fifty people sleeping in the room and someone was going to and from the privy at almost any hour. The woodsman was snoring, a horrifying sound that was abnormally affected by the man's misshapen throat, or so Jamus imagined, as were a number of others with less obvious reasons for their nightly disturbances. Somewhere a child coughed, and in another corner of the room a woman sneezed. Jamus found nothing surprising about any of that, not with the coldness of the weather.

As he listened Jamus considered the room as he had seen it before the last lantern was extinguished. Gran had given up on separating the men from the women when whole families began using the shelter and demanded that they be left together. Because of that Gran slept on the cot at the woodsman's feet and Jamus lay to the big man's right. Not that the rows of beds in the room could all be called true cots. Most were makeshift affairs with old blankets sewn into a bag and stuffed with straw, spread over a pile of firewood to keep it off the ground. The woodsman had one of the few that had legs and space to place anything underneath and his was occupied by a chamber pot. The furnishings of the room were few; mostly firewood stacked before the few windows if logs could be called furnishings, and the belongings of the refugees were piled haphazardly wherever people could find a spot on the floor. Walking between the beds was difficult if not impossible without tripping over something, but those who had been sleeping here each night were becoming better at doing so. Just then Jamus heard the sound that awoke him; the muffled curse of a man.

Sitting up as quietly as he was able, the straw in his mattress was fresh and creaked when he moved, Jamus squinted towards the main doorway, looking for some sign of the visitor. He knew that no one who had been staying in the hospital would be using such language around the many children in the room; Gran had made it very clear that that would not be tolerated and switched one teamster who forgot. Unfortunately the darkness remained all but absolute.

Relaxing, Jamus allowed his vision to remain unfocused, staring off into the blackness and waiting for some movement to draw his eye. It worked; in no time he detected a wave of darkness moving against a deeper darkness; not sight, exactly, but it was successful in telling him where the newcomer was. In this instance it revealed that the man was about mid-way between Jamus and the main door.

The man cursed again; not speaking a word exactly, but a sound made in exasperation nonetheless. A few more unidentifiable sounds followed before a truly significant noise occurred; the solid thump of someone's toe striking a stick of firewood. The curse that followed was unmistakable.

"Would ya shut up, people are trying to sleep," growled a voice from the darkness.

"There ain't no more beds, get out of here," stated another.

"Ain't nothing here worth stealing either," came a third.

"I kind of hope someone tries too," growled a deep baritone from somewhere near the middle of the room. "I've been itching for a fight since we got cooped up in this town."

Accompanied by a chorus of similar comments, the new arrival apparently changed his mind about staying in the hospital, if the string of curses that followed his exit was any indication. Jamus followed the man's progress by sound; tripping over a boot, kicking someone's bed and the clatter of a chamber pot tipping over. A blast of deeper cold was followed by the slamming of the main door and the general laughter of those woke by the man's entrance.

"Wonder what he wanted?" questioned the baritone.

"He? There were two of them," replied a woman. "They passed on either side of my bed."

"Probably got cold sleeping on the ground, decided to try and find a bed," offered a different woman's voice.

"Good luck," grouched yet another man. "I'm already sleeping on the floor. I'm freezing!"

Another laugh rippled about the room and Jamus joined the general population as he settled back to sleep. Not everyone awoke; Gran merely mumbled a single 'like as not' without waking. The big woodsman, however, was awake although he continued to snore.

"Your fake snore is quite unconvincing," Jamus whispered low enough that only his neighbor could hear. In return the woodsman gave the throaty rasp Jamus had identified as the best laugh the man could manage.

Almost Jamus drifted back to sleep; his aching back and hands made getting there just a little more difficult than it otherwise would have been so when the piece of bark struck his cheek he was still in that half-asleep, half-awake state where he remained conscious, but was completely relaxed and unable to react. Looking around helped him not at all; it was of course still too dark to see, but then another bit of bark struck him in the nose and his scattered wits returned.

The bark had come from his left; the woodsman must have picked the bits off the firewood piled beside his cot. A third bit hit him, this time in the throat, so he threw back a bit of his own to let the man know that he was awake. But why he was needed to be awake he didn't know; until he heard the voices.

Muffled, the speakers were obviously not inside the building. Straining to hear Jamus picked up a few stray words. There were at least two men speaking, and they were trying not to be heard. It took some time for him to pick out the direction the voices were coming from; and he wasn't surprised when he realized they were coming from outside.

There were only a few windows in the room, but one of them happened to be just beyond the woodsman's bed. They were typical frontier windows; no pains of glass had as of yet been imported here so the openings were just wooden shutters over a square hole. Staring that direction accomplished nothing; there was just no light there to reveal anything. Unless Jamus was badly mistaken, and overhearing things people were trying to whisper was one of the skills a courtier must develop, at least one of the voices belonged to the man who had been cursing.

"This corner, I'm sure of it," the man said, his voice as fleeting as the faintest breath of wind. "The old woman is right through here."

"And now what? We can't break through these shutters without waking up half the town," came the reply. Silence followed.

"We'll have to come back, do it tomorrow or the next day."

"He's not going to like it."

"Yeah well I wouldn't like to get my head chopped off for three bits of silver either!"

The two men continued to argue, their voices dropping so that even the concentrating Jamus could no longer hear them. Whatever they said made neither man happy but eventually they reached a consensus.

"Come on, let's get out of here then," one stated.

"It's about time; I can't even feel my feet anymore."

"We do this tomorrow then? We're agreed?"

"Right, tomorrow."

# Chapter Seventeen

The guard always changed two hours past midnight. It was a tradition among the Aldrigal Dragons, the King's personal bodyguard, and that was the way it had been done for decades. To say that it was common knowledge might be a stretch, but it was child's play for the spies of Firth to learn of it. That's why the first Quargs climbed the wall at an hour past midnight; the guards on duty would be at their most tired, looking inward towards their relief than outwards for attackers, and the oncoming group would still be in their beds. It worked like a charm.

If the matter had been left up to the Quargs they would have attacked the king's summer palace as soon as they were near it, but thanks to the Were 'advisor' sent with them the humanoid attack was precisely on time. As they had been told the walls of the palace were ornamental, in reality they were little more than a fence of wrought iron with an elevated walkway that kept the guards a head higher than the man-sized fence itself, and the nimble Quargs sent first had no trouble scaling it. A few slit throats later and the gate stood wide for the main force.

Quargs admired bravery and they saw it in abundance that night. Singing among the humanoids consisted mostly of religious chants but a few times each year they sang guttural tales of foes slain and bravery witnessed, and more than few tales telling of the Dragons would be born this night. The men fought like they were possessed with demons and threw themselves at the Quargs wearing nothing more than nightshirts, sometimes even less, and bearing any weapon they could find. Individual Quargs died from skulls crushed by chairs, chamber pots, and firewood or found themselves spitted on pokers or knives from the kitchens. One unlucky warrior slipped on a freshly waxed floor and broke his neck, but the humans died quickly.

The floors of the barracks ran red with the blood of these brave men but in the end they died. Here and there a handful of servants made their way out a little known service gate or climbed the fence to freedom, but a sizeable portion of those were hunted down by the wolves kept ravenous for that very duty. Those who did not die immediately were soon dispatched, once the looting was complete, and few were the humans from the palace who survived the bloody night.

For the most part the Quargs found the palace to be filled with easy prey for unarmed and unarmored the knights had little beyond their zeal to overcome the spears and axes of the attackers. Only in that portion of the mansion called the Royal Suite did the Quargs die faster than the defenders. There the guards were few but not surprised thanks to the screams of those who had died without. These men gave ground unwillingly, their shining blades carrying spells of sharpness that passed like butter through wooden shields and flesh alike. Servants in that wing joined the knights and threw vases at the attackers, or used brooms to trip them to be butchered by the knights. Quarg bodies far outnumbered those of the fully armed and armored knights and it was only by the press of numbers that the guards were finally pulled down. Offers of ransom were ignored as the men were pounded into jelly within their gleaming suits of plate. None of the Quargs understood the human language anyway.

A statue was used to batter down the massive doors of the throne room; taking longer to accomplish than taking the palace had, simply because the Quargs could not figure out how to open the complex latch. Food stores in the kitchen were stolen as quickly as individual Quargs could stuff the provisions into their pockets or packs. Anything that looked remotely like a precious metal; and the palace had those in abundance, was taken off, torn down, or otherwise confiscated by the victorious looters. Being Quargs there were instances where valuable paintings or priceless tapestries were burned or trampled into the floor to obtain something worth mere coppers but all the invaders had their pockets full before the sun broke the horizon.

One last room remained undefiled by the Quargs. It sat at the end of the main hallway of the Royal Suite and had so far withstood the battering of axes and hammers. Obviously the door carried a powerful charm and the Quargs were at a loss as to how to open it. As the hours passed their shamans had had no success either. Finally the Were was summoned for even the dimmest of Quargs realized that the king of Aldrigal himself had to be behind that door.

"Fools and simpletons," the Were, whose name was Mol, rasped. His half-man half-wolf form made it difficult to speak but he persevered because he felt that the Quargs deserved it. With all the magical weapons among the Aldrigal Dragons, he had felt it prudent to remain in his rugged Were form than to be taken by surprise as a human. Only shamans stood between him and the door now and the Were didn't even bother to push them out of his way as he bulled through the throng. Behind him came the Signaler; the only one detailed to come with the Quargs, and the unpleasant woman followed him closely, giggling under her breath as she always did.

Mol shouldered past a last shaman, interrupting the fellow's prayer in mid syllable so that he mispronounced the name of some Quarg deity as he tumbled to the floor. Compared to the other Quargs serving

Firth, Mol had been the oldest in years when he received the Curse but was near the bottom of the list in terms of time spent as a Were. His fur had patches of gray at the chest and hackles, and individuals of the same color were spread liberally about the rest of his pelt. He was no fool, however, and did not immediately touch the magical door.

"What do you think?" he snapped, not bothering to look back at the Signaler. She knew who he was speaking to, however, and stepped up next to him before she replied.

"I think it's a door," she giggled, her eyes bulging out in feigned innocence. The woman was ugly, as thin as a willow switch, and kept a round circle shaved on the peak of her head. In addition to her constant giggling, the woman also sneezed regularly.

Looking down at the woman to be certain that she knew he wasn't joking, Mol growled. "Is the door magic or not?"

Missing his hint completely the Signaler giggled, then sneezed, then giggled again before replying.

"No, but it might have magic on it somewhere."

Growling again Mol grabbed the woman by the arm and shoved her forward. He loathed touching her as it made even his Cursed skin crawl, but he was growing tired of her endless games.

"Open the door or I'll kill you," he stated simply.

The king had been found nowhere in the palace. If he wasn't in this room then he wasn't here, and Mol's latest intelligence report said that he most assuredly was. He wasn't sure that he could kill the woman, he had no idea of what a Signaler's powers truly were, but she was supposed to help him with any magical obstacles and he had no other way to force her cooperation. With a final giggle she complied with his demand.

She studied the door, standing as closely to it as she could without coming into contact with the metal. Not for the first time Mol thought that the woman must be near sighted. The door was very ornate, with swirls and sigils inlaid in silver on the steel door. It would take two strong men just to open it and, remembering the hours lost by the Quargs in battering down the unlocked throne room doors, Mol wondered if any of the foolish Quargs had even tried to turn the handle.

"Has anyone touched the door?" the Signaler asked, peering around at the gathered shamans. None replied though Mol knew that a couple of them spoke the human tongue.

"Do you want someone to touch it?" growled Mol.

"Not necessarily," the Signaler replied, returning to her inspection of the door. "But if someone already had, it would tell me if there were surface traps set to trigger when an unauthorized person came in contact with it. It would have saved me some time, that's all."

Wordlessly Mol turned to the assembled Quargs and chose the

closest one, grabbing the shaman up by the back of the neck. With his Cursed strength, Mol was easily able to lift the fellow with one hand. Shouldering the woman out of the way and ignoring the protests of the shaman, he casually pressed the Quarg's face against the door and then dragged him all over the portal, ensuring that his face remained in contact over the entire surface.

"Nothing," he commented, dropping the bleeding Quarg to the floor. The shaman's face was cut from the metallic edges and he was bleeding profusely from his flattened nose.

Giggling wildly the woman spun in a circle before returning to the door; this time she didn't hesitate to place her hands directly on the surface and promptly sneezed on it.

Closing her eyes the Signaler began chanting wordlessly and continued doing so for some time. Eventually she did open her eyes just long enough to sneeze once but then returned to her task. Then, moving so suddenly she almost frightened the Quargs into a stampede, she leaped back and began screaming at the door in a language Mol didn't understand, threw a handful of straw at the portal that burst into flame upon contact, and sneezed three times in rapid succession before kicking it solidly at the base. With an audible click the latch tripped and the door swung outward and remained slightly ajar.

"Ow," she stated proudly, giggling as she waved Mol towards the door while attempting to rub her sore toe.

With the weapons of the Aldrigal Dragons in mind, Mol shoved a nearby armful of Quarg warriors towards the door, noticing as he did that the shamans had already evacuated the hallway. Although they were fearful of what lay ahead the warriors were more fearful of what stood behind them so they went; easing the door open with the points of several spears to compensate for the weight of the portal.

The room beyond was opulent beyond Mol's simple imagination. The floors were thick with carpet, the walls painted with fantastical scenes from legend. Almost as large as the throne room, the room was dominated by a four poster bed large enough to sleep a dozen people. The furniture scattered about was functional but just as easily qualified as art so amazing they were in both form and materials. The ceiling was vaulted and gemstones sparkled from every surface, twinkling like stars in the reflected light of the oil lamps mounted on the pillars of the outer walls that supported it. There were six people in the room and all were clustered on or near the massive bed.

Mol waited until a handful of Quargs had preceded him before he entered the bedchamber. No surprise lay to either side of the door and the room had only one other exit; a smaller door that probably led to a dressing chamber or closet. To either side of the bed's foot stood two of the Aldrigal Dragons; their full plate armor gleamed and the soft humming coming from their glaives, not to mention the ease with which the men held the huge blades, warned Mol that they were magical. On the bed itself three people clustered around a fourth; the King of Aldrigal.

Enjoying the gasps of fear at the sight of him, Mol strolled leisurely towards the bed, never really taking his focus from the knights even as he looked at the king. The warriors were nervous but resolved to their fate, and the glaives barely trembled at his approach. Mol felt an uncommon surge of fear at the sight of them; these men just might be able to kill him. He kept closing until he saw the knights begin to shift their feet, and then paused there to speak; he was here to take the king alive.

Elderly, propped up on pillows to keep his head high enough to see his abductors, the King of Aldrigal gazed regally upon the Were. As the bed was quite high, the king's eyes were on a level with Mol's chest and somehow the man was able to give the appearance of looking down upon the Were. The man may have been old, but Mol had no doubt that the king still felt that he was in command of the situation; all his life he had been the unquestioned ruler with every whim obeyed, so how could he feel otherwise?

To either side of the king were a young woman and a small boy; family by the manner of their dress. The woman was beautiful with raven hair and full painted lips. Mol was doubtful she'd even left her teens yet. The boy was perhaps ten and was trying to look brave even as he clutched the king's nightshirt with both fists. These were members of the royal family; probably grandchildren or great grandchildren of the king.

"You are my prisoner," Mol stated simply. The king didn't respond.

From his place standing near the head of the bed a portly man of fifty stepped out, nervously circling the Dragon to Mol's right in order to stand before the Were. He was frightened, Mol could smell it on him, but his face showed no sign of it. He was dressed in an expensive black suit of woolen pants, short vest, and coat complete with tails than dropped to below the knee. A servant, perhaps, but one high in the king's confidence.

Clearing his throat the servant squared his shoulders and did his best to stare Mol straight in the eye despite being a head shorter.

"His Majesty has commanded that I speak on his behalf," the man stated in the same tone of voice he likely used to announce noble visitors to the throne room.

Mol laughed; a short, harsh bark that went well with his wolf-like visage.

"Very well; please inform his majesty that he is my prisoner."

Apparently the man had already been coached as to what to say because he did not hesitate or look to the king for guidance before replying.

"His Majesty recognizes that you and your army have defeated his guardsman and presently hold control of the palace. As is your right under the laws of pillage he grants your soldiers the right to carry away whatever valuables they wish, holding only in reserve the jewels of state. In return His Majesty expects your warriors to behave themselves in a civilized manner, to pardon the non-combatants and the royal family, and to leave the palace in peace before the sun has set upon this day."

Whistling in respect, a difficult thing to do in Were form, Mol shook his head at the man's audacity. Imagine ordering the group of Quargs to take their plunder and leave without killing, or worse, the women and children. And to do so in such a haughty manner; almost as if the king were granting a gift to them and was not at their mercy, was something to marvel at.

"Perhaps your king does not understand; we are not a band of raiders, we are an invasion force. Your king is my prisoner and will live, or die, at my whim. What the Quargs take from this palace, including the royal family, are not his to decide."

From the red flush rising in the king's face Mol could see that the old man was getting angry, but it was the servant who responded.

"His majesty's person, along with those of the Princess Tetraphe and Prince Galvin, are not subject to your whims. His majesty will concede your ownership of the palace and will vacate the premises straight away. In return for his safe conduct he will advise his armies to be merciful when dealing with you."

After a brief dramatic pause the man continued. "As you can see; His Majesty is being more than fair. Once his armies hear of your attack they will speed here with all due dispatch and, well, you cannot hope that your little band of Quargs can survive such an attack."

Again Mol smiled. How could he not in the face of such arrogance, or if not that, bravery? The king still found it unacceptable that he should be a prisoner; his world view simply could not fathom it.

Turning his head slightly Mol barked a command in the Quarg language and spent the next few moments smiling at the king; tongue lolling from his snout and incisors in plain view. Presently the sound of iron-shod boots were heard and after the warriors in the hallway made room, a dozen Quargs marched through the door and lined up to either side. Lifting their crossbows they took careful aim at the now even more nervous Dragons and awaited Mol's command.

"Tell your king that he is my prisoner, as are the rest of his family, and only by cooperating fully with me will any of them see the light of another day."

Finally the servant showed a chink in his armor. Glancing nervously back towards his king, he awaited some command about what to do now.

Then, surprising the servant and Mol, the king spoke.

"The King of Aldrigal will never surrender to a commoner nor one of Cursed blood. If that is your offer than you may kill us all now, we shall not beg. Speak to me, beast; who is your master?"

Pulling himself to his full height Mol allowed the change to grip him. His muscles bulged, then receded as ligaments and joints popped and crackled. The pain was intense, as it always was, but not the exquisite, almost joyful, pain that changing from human to Were brought. Nude he may have been but Mol felt that the king might be more willing to negotiate with him in human form.

Not a sound did the Were make as he changed, and he was gratified at the horrified expressions in the barely visible eyes of the Dragons as well as the terrified whimpers of the children. The servant paled visibly and backed up three steps; hoping that his presence near the Were was finished now that the king was speaking for himself but without a command to verify it he was too well trained to move as far away as he wished. The king himself made not a sound, but the slight widening of his eyes and the disgust that lifted the corners of his mouth told Mol that he had made the impression that he wanted.

"I am of common birth, it is true," he announced, staring directly at the king. "But he I serve is of noble blood and of a lineage as old as yours."

"I do not recognize the nobility of any Quarg, much less that of a Were."

"Just take him," whispered the Signaler as he joined him. She combined the advice with a combination giggle and sneeze that should have hurt. Her voice was too low to be heard by anyone else but the king's face reddened to see someone speak when he was talking. Such an insult could result in imprisonment.

Mol ignored her. "He that I serve is neither Quarg nor Were. He is as human as you and leads his own nation; a nation now as powerful as your own. Indeed, he rules his own in addition to yours, for our attack was far more widespread than the taking of this one palace. Even as we speak our troops hold your capitol and prepare to march on your lesser cities; the nation of Aldrigal will soon be a province of he that I serve, and your family will either submit to that rule or die."

The king's rage was growing by the moment but despite his age he was far from feeble minded. A politician to his core, he knew when to accept a loss and began planning for future victories.

"Then name your master and if he is what you claim I shall surrender myself to you against that happy day when the men of Aldrigal shall topple him in my favor, or in that of my heir."

Mol nearly howled in glee, and would have had he been in wolf form. Making the old man submit with words rather than teeth seemed more fitting somehow; and the Were knew that the presence of the royal grandchildren had a lot to do with the easy capitulation.

"My master is the unquestioned ruler of the mighty nation that is Firth."

Comically surprised, the king gave a single dry chuckle.

"Firth? That pitiful little backwoods duchy dares to invade mighty Aldrigal? Your duke may have surprised us and taken me but he cannot hope to withstand the counter attack of our armies. My son will wear your pelt as a cloak, beast-man. You have that to look forward to."

Turning to the Quargs Mol gave an order, and then turned back to face the king so he could look into the man's eyes as his last remaining guards died. The armor of the Dragons was the finest made, and carried magic to make it stronger and lighter. But when six bolts, fired at such close range from crossbows as powerful as these, struck each of the men at least one was destined to get through. With a pair of matching grunts both Dragons collapsed to a scream by the princess.

"We are finished with the insults, old man. I command here now and the Duke of Firth is your sovereign. Submit now of your own free will or I will take you."

For some time the two men glared at one another but the king had no room to negotiate. Tears filled the king's eyes as he finally spoke.

"I submit to the Duke of Firth."

# Chapter Eighteen

"Two dead men were found in an alley this morning," announced Vert, ever proud to be the bearer of news. "They were in a barrel with their throats cut; looked like someone used a thin knife, then stuffed them in there so no one would notice for awhile."

The redhead sat on a cot speaking to Gran and Tomo, staying as far as he could from where the woodsman sat three cots away. He was thin and a year older than Albrim, having been friends with Gran's grandson since they were small. The son of a tanner killed in the same Were attack that had cost Albrim his arm, Vert still stank of the business despite the weeks he had been away from his home, living as a refugee. His family had been one of those who followed Tomo when the man had warned of the approaching army. Vert and Tomo had been the only two Gran trusted when she faked Albrim's death.

"Trouble caused by strong drink, like as not," Gran stated as she double tied the straps on the pack resting on the floor between her feet. "Men and the trouble they find," she quoted. Gran seemed to know every old proverb and folk saying there was. Vert had secretly maintained that her knowledge of them was simply earned; she was so old that it had been she that invented them all to begin with.

Tomo leaned forward to shake the younger man's hand. "My thanks again, Vert, for looking after my family."

Vert blushed. He was proud to be trusted with such a task. At eighteen he was being treated like a man, something he had longed for, for many years. The death of his father and subsequent tasks performed for Gran had forced him to mature quickly. His recent marriage and now pregnant wife had brought on even more. Now he was nervous about being able to live up to their trust.

"I'll see to them like they were my own family," he stated solemnly.

"We know that Vert, you're a good boy," Gran smiled, not mentioning that since Vert was a cousin of Tomo's wife and Tomo was a cousin of Vert's wife, that in many ways they were his family. Turning back to Tomo her smile died.

"And you, haring off on some fool adventure when you should be here caring for your own! I taught you better than that, like as not."

Tomo acted chagrined. It had only taken him a few minutes of protesting to convince Gran to let him come along; and he couldn't have changed her mind if she hadn't truly wanted him to accompany her.

"You can't go alone, Gran, and Vert has a pregnant wife. Our other friend," he indicated the big woodsman, "can't travel yet, so it'll have to be me. You'd never find your way through the wilds without a tracker."

Gran sniffed. "I've been finding my own way since long before you were born, boy, and will continue to do so as needed in the future, like as not."

Making sure that his smile was only to himself Tomo did not reply. Again Gran had pointedly not refused to allow him to come with her despite her argument.

"Mayor Lauder didn't try to stop you from going?" Vert asked.

"That fool doesn't command us," Gran scoffed.

"He did suggest that we stay here in safety, but he's of the same mind that we are; the Quargs aren't coming this far south," Tomo said, winking at Vert behind Gran's head. Both were thinking the same thing; there was no way the Mayor could have stopped Gran from doing whatever she wanted.

At that point Jamus entered the room; he was dressed better than he had been since the carriage and the clothing he wore practically fit him. Rugged and stout rather than the silks he probably would have preferred, the garments looked warm and new. He was obviously dressed for travel and looked happier than he had for some time, though the loss of his wife was still visible in his haunted eyes.

"I've got the supplies, Gran," he said. The coins he had salvaged from his wife's body had been mostly silver but there had been some of gold as well. Despite the high prices the refugees had forced upon Vicksville's economy his money had easily provided everything Gran had needed with plenty left over to see them to a city. He'd even managed a few twists of tobacco for Tomo and, at Gran's insistence, provided Vert with a small emergency fund as well.

"You found us a packhorse?" she demanded, fixing her best eye upon the noble.

"Yes, he's not much to look at but the woman who sold him to me says he's strong and tireless. I wouldn't wish to ride him in any parades but he'll do, I suspect."

"You go on outside, I'll be out in a moment," Gran said, accepting the noble's word. Vicksville was not rich in horseflesh, so they were happy to have found any mount for sale. Obediently the three men left the hospital, leaving Gran alone with the woodsman.

Dragging a short stool over to his bedside Gran sat near the man's head and slipped one hand up to check the man's forehead for fever. Finding none she smiled at him and kissed him gently on the cheek.

"I'm sorry we didn't get to spend more time together," she whispered. "I've truly missed you."

Not being able to speak the woodsman reached up to grab Gran's hand and held it tightly. Tears were in both their eyes. Releasing his grip the man went through a complex set of motions with his hands.

"No, you cannot come with us; you're just too badly injured," Gran stated, this time loud enough for the two men lounging near the door to hear. "I'll come back for you in two weeks; you'll be ready to travel by then so long as you don't try to walk too much."

Smiling thinly the woodsman again made motions with his hands.

Keeping her voice low again Gran replied, "I don't know if they know who you really are but they do know you're the man from the wanted poster." She shook her head in wonder. "After all you've done for people you've still managed to make yourself a wanted criminal under two different names."

He laughed, speaking again with his hands.

"Albrim did? Well I guess he had to, with you two not be able to talk. What name did he give you?"

Again he motioned, this time with fingers only.

"Mute? That's it? I guess it worked well enough, like as not," Gran smiled. "He's a good boy, and you're a good boy. I'm sorry to leave you here."

Mute shook his head, waving away her words before signing again.

"I know, you did what you could for him and no one could have done more. But now he's beyond your help, and beyond anyone else's for that matter save my own. This is something I have to do."

Sadly he signed again, pointing to his arm at the end.

"Yes, Borel was too good a man to die so needlessly. We spoke about you often; but not around Albrim. We felt that your secret was safer the fewer of us that knew it."

Mute nodded, his eyes still wet and sad with understanding. Taking her hand again he pressed his lips to it.

Gran kissed him again, lovingly stroking his face as she did so.

Any tenderness Gran had demonstrated inside the building was gone by the time she went outside. The others were all gathered about a distinctly sway-backed nag Gran was surprised hadn't fallen over from age while waiting. The provisions packed on its back had been stripped off and an embarrassed Jamus stood helplessly watching as Tomo repacked it. Vert was laughing good naturedly.

"Don't feel too bad, I probably couldn't have done any better," Vert was saying, clapping Jamus on the back.

"It's just that the load was uneven, and would have caused the horse a lot of discomfort," Tomo was explaining. "You have to balance out the weight..." he paused, noticing Gran approaching. "Almost ready to go, Gran," he finished, glancing at her injured leg disapprovingly. She had removed her own splint that very morning despite the warnings of the other healers and to the surprise of them all was able to walk on it.

Gran gave the horse a good looking over and decided that the nobleman had been taken. No matter what he paid for the animal, it would have been too much.

"Poor thing," she stated, patting the horse gently on the nose. "You've had a tough life of hard work, like as not, and all I can offer you is a place to rot along the road somewhere."

"I take it you're not happy with the horse either," Jamus said, wincing. Vert and Tomo both chuckled.

"I suppose he'll do until he drops dead," Gran grouched.

"Probably somewhere around the gate," quipped Tomo.

"Oh I believe it'll make it much further than that," added Vert. "Perhaps even all the way outside the walls."

Jamus blushed furiously. "Look, I didn't have enough money for a proper animal and I only gave two bits for this one."

Tomo seemed on the verge of another comment but Gran cut him off.

"It'll do; we have to get going. 'A beggar sups his soup even when it's cold,'" she stated, quoting the Jackdog story that saw the hungry creature trick a town into feeding him despite a local famine.

After saying farewell to Vert the three men walked ahead, leading the ancient horse and leaving Gran to follow along behind. Tomo's wife stood watching them go; she and her husband had already said their goodbyes and he was afraid to meet her eyes in case he began crying again.

"I'll bring him back to you dear," Gran said, taking the woman's hand. "You know it's needful."

She smiled through her tears. "I know Gran. You know best," she added before moving back into the crowd. Gran wasn't certain that the woman believed her own words.

"It's needful," Gran repeated, her heart breaking as she watched the woman leave.

Turning back intending to hurry, she soon realized that the poor horse walked even slower than she did with a sore leg. It took some time but eventually they managed to work their way through the throng and out the gates.

Gran was silently brooding, Tomo was still sniffling, the horse was staggering, and only Jamus seemed glad to be leaving the town. His feet were already beginning to hurt and he despised the thought of walking all the way to Skallist but was happily explaining how wonderful just the thought of escaping so many unwashed peasant bodies would be. He kept up his patter so long that Gran eventually gave him a stripe with her switch, her walking staff clutched in the other hand as if threatening to use it as well.

Each wrapped up in their private thoughts the three didn't look back as they circled the town and left it towards the south. Even if they had it was doubtful that they would have noticed the one man among the throng of people watching them leave, but Burstis kept them in sight as long as he could.

Then he followed.

# Chapter Nineteen

Easing back into the warm water Lionel von Firth, the Duke of Firth, gave a contented sigh. A few more moments in the bath and he would have a nice massage; all the better to relax him before he went to visit his wife.

The fireplace roared as the servants did all they could to combat any errant drafts that might spoil the duke's mood and they were all dripping with sweat as a result of their activities. He was in an extraordinarily good mood this day and they desperately wanted to maintain it. With the monetary problems their small independent duchy had been experiencing in recent years it was not often the duke relaxed enough to be cordial to his servants. Today he was being overly generous with his praise.

News of the invasion was going very well; only last night Dirk, his main liaison with his less than legal activities, had brought him a report from General Handrick. Aldrigal City had fallen as planned!

An oil lantern above and to the left of the fireplace suddenly flickered and went out. One of a dozen similar lamps in the room its light was not missed and it held no more significance than any other, except to the duke.

"Leave me, please, I wish some quiet," he said, smiling towards the servants as they immediately gathered their things and left the room. It wasn't an unusual thing for the duke to request. Their lack of suspicion and curiosity were among the primary reasons they had been chosen for their jobs.

Once the last servant had left and the door was closed tightly behind them a panel in the wall slid away to reveal the diminutive Dirk. He was nondescript and dressed only slightly better than a small time merchant. Formally an assassin, the man had worked hard to develop his appearance into that of someone easily overlooked and rarely remembered. Stepping into the room he closed the secret door behind him and approached the duke.

Keeping his voice pitched low the duke greeted him. "Ah Dirk, good to see you. I hope you have arrived with even more good news for me?"

Dirk bowed, unwilling to task the duke's good mood despite the fact that he did, indeed, have good news to share.

"A rider arrived only moments ago, my lord, bringing news of the successful sacking of the King's Summer Palace; the King of Aldrigal is officially your guest."

Careful not to let out a whoop of joy that would be difficult to explain to anyone listening, the duke instead stood to his feet, heedless of the water splashing onto the floor, and raised his fist in triumph.

"How many other members of the royal family did we take?" he whispered.

Dirk very nearly smiled. "Two, your grace. Princess Tetraphe and Prince Galvin were visiting the king at the time of the attack. Prince Maunder and Prince Desmond died in the attack."

Lionel eased back into the water, humming as he pondered the news. "So we captured two grandchildren and killed another. Who is Prince Desmond?"

As ever Dirk was ready with the answer. "A cousin, my lord. Twenty third in line for the throne and a member of the Aldrigal Dragons; the king's personal guards."

"Fine, one less royal is a good stroke for us. Any sign of the Crown Prince?"

"No, your grace, Prince Holister is still out of the country, acting as emissary to Fadrimor."

Waving the issue away Lionel leaned back into the tub, allowing the warm water to rise up to his chin. "He is of no consequence; he'll make an acceptable puppet if I choose to have him rule my new lands for me but I'm not worried about any trouble he might make," the duke said, careful not allow the bathwater to splash into his mouth. "There are other Aldrigalian royals I am more concerned about. Any word on the other family members?"

"Yes, your grace. As you already know six members of the royal family were killed or detained in Aldrigal, including Prince Manix who now awaits your pleasure in the city guard-pit. Since we spoke last I have received a message saying that the Princess Abigail was captured trying to escape the city dressed as a victim of the blood plague."

Despite the warmth of the room and the water the duke shivered at the thought of a blood plague victim. The disease was extremely unwholesome; victims in the later stages of the disease were covered in large boils that occasionally burst, spraying plague-tainted blood into the air. Those suffering from the ailment were dressed in thick red robes by the church to warn people to stay well away.

"Abigail? Very good; she was one of those I was most concerned about. That family only has a few stout hearts among them, and I want to make sure we remove them to discourage any revolts," Lionel explained. Not something he normally bothered to do for an underling.

Dirk bowed again, unsure how to react to such an uncommon thing.

"So how many royals are still at large?"

Dirk pretended to consult a stack of parchment even though he knew the answer.

"Counting Crown Prince Holister there are seven members of the king's immediately family not yet dead or under your control. Of his extended family there are at least twelve others plus a handful of young children."

"Fine, all goes well then. What of the invasion itself; have any serious issues cropped up?"

"No, my lord, nothing major as of yet. There continues to be some rioting in Aldrigal City, but most of that is being caused by your mercenary troops. The palace is quiet because the Quargs butchered everyone living save the king and his two grandchildren mentioned earlier."

"Are the Quargs still reliable for the next phase of the plan?"

Nodding, Dirk shifted the parchments around until he found the one he wanted. "General Handrick still decries the lack of commitment from the Quargs; apparently he still has not received all the warriors he was promised. A sizeable number of them are still searching the forest for this 'Keon-din' they so despise. The palace fell with reasonably light casualties, so the Were in command of the Quargs feel that enough of them remain to complete their duties despite those that deserted once they had their loot. He is also hopeful that more Quargs will join his forces when they hear of the plunder the others have taken."

"Fine. What exactly are the next targets?"

Again Dirk shifted the parchments about, this time removing and unrolling one that turned out to be a map of Aldrigal. Dirk used it to point out the various locations as he spoke.

"The Quargs are at the summer palace, here, and while they maintain a sizeable force here along the Skallist road they will send a portion of their strength to sweep the southern wilds while the main body assaults the eastern border towns here, here, and here. General Handrick will leave a sizeable garrison at Aldrigal under General Intona and will proceed with the remainder to capture the city and river port of Nazrigal. Once he has it under his control and garrisoned he will begin sweeping the area to the north, stamping out any resistance he chances upon and pressing men into service. With those soldiers and the levies taken from Aldrigal City, he hopes to lay siege to the fortress of Taramont and so control the most likely rally point of any Aldrigalian resistance."

Happily the duke studied the map, peering at obscure references on it long after the former assassin had finished speaking. The bold part of the plan was past; now it was time to be even bolder.

"Handrick believes he can take the fortress despite the winter weather?"

"Yes my lord; he believes that he has sufficient resources to circumvent most of the defenses and so take it swiftly. He plans to winter there."

"I assume the treasuries of both the city and the palace are on their way back to Firth?"

"Yes, your grace, and the call for more mercenary companies has been sent out now that the need for secrecy is past. By the time your enemies can hope to respond to the news that most of your army is across the mountains, we should have a sizeable replacement force in place here."

"And no other nations have so far responded to the invasion?"

"Nothing has been heard as of yet, my lord. Likely they are only now becoming aware of it and most will believe it a false rumor and wait for it to be verified before sending emissaries to you."

"Sounds reasonable Dirk. I agree with your assessment. What of our own loyal nobility? Have any of them noticed our victory?"

"Again, my lord, I believe that the answer is no. Surely they will within a day or two, but not before. Your plan was very daring, your grace, and has, from all indications, taken everyone by surprise."

Lionel smiled brightly as he pondered all that he had heard. Aldrigal City and the King being in his control were major steps towards pacifying the kingdom, as was the taking of the treasuries. The fact remained that Aldrigal could still field ten times the number of men that he could if they had someone or something to rally around. The northern cities were still untouched and his hopes were that some of them would take the opportunity to declare themselves independent, and so deny Aldrigal its remaining strength. Where was the infamous Jackdog, fabled savior of Aldrigal, now?

# Chapter Twenty

Sometimes fate intervened on one's behalf, and other times against you. For Burstis it seemed as if he was finally making a gain against the poor luck he'd been having. First he had discovered Gran hiding in the village, despite the failure of his hired killers to take her there, and now he had discovered a sizeable band of Quargs at a most convenient time. Not that the leader of the band had been entirely happy to see him.

"My apologies sir," he had growled that first day around a mouthful of protruding tusks. "There is said to be a rogue Were in the woods around here; a real beast they say. We were supposed to look for its tracks while we scouted so, you gave us a start when he you came out of the woods."

Burstis didn't bother to chuckle with the Were. He'd almost had to kill the fellow, so violent had been the war band's reaction to his appearance. To prevent any such accidents he had approached them in Were form, trusting in the treaty between the Quargs and his master. Not that they could have harmed him; but he wanted them along for his next plan. Now, after two days together spent moving parallel to Gran's route, the Quargs still acted uneasy in his presence.

"A rogue Were? Has anyone seen what he looked like?" Burstis had asked at that first meeting, not even bothering to add the obvious 'and lived' to his question.

"Big Were, brown fur mostly, and only one foreleg," was the reply.

That told Burstis all he needed to know; the youth from the carriage was indeed in the area, likely waiting on Gran to leave the village. Burstis didn't believe for a moment that the boy was still wild; likely he just liked killing Quargs after their attack on the old woman. Perhaps he thought he could convince the humanoids to stay away from the area, and so protect her in that manner as well. It was good information to know; he was going to set up an ambush to kill Gran once and for all, and knowing that she had a Were protector was a valuable piece to have. That made the Quargs even more valuable; they could kill the humans easily enough but Burstis would have to deal with the Were. And while he was doing that the humans might interfere or once again escape. He was tired of chasing that woman around the wilderness.

Burstis had no doubt that he could handle the other Were. He was experienced in Were to Were combat and was in the prime of his life. The boy, on the other hand, could not have suffered the Curse more than a couple of years and would likely have difficulty controlling himself. Plus, being so young, he would not have the strength to deal with Burstis and that was even discounting the missing arm. Yes, Burstis felt confident that he could handle the boy.

"How many warriors do you have? And how many wolves?" he asked the Quarg leader, having already forgotten the fellow's name.

"I have this many hands plus this of warriors," the Quarg stated, holding up four fingers and then three. "And I have two hands and two of wolves," he stated, proud that he could actually count to two, "and one of them is the big kind."

Twenty-three Quargs and a dozen wolves? More than enough to deal with the problem, Burstis decided. It had been the scent of the wolves that had attracted him to the Quarg band, particularly that of the larger one. Breeding them to such great size had largely been his idea, though he had had nothing to do with the actual husbandry. If you could breed larger and stronger horses, why not do the same with wolves? They were smarter as well.

"Have your scouts crossed their trail yet?"

"Yes sir, they have," the Quarg stated, dropping to a squat and clearing away the frozen leaves from the ground. In the eight days that had passed since Burstis had left Vicksville it had snowed four times but nothing had accumulated yet. Using the point of his rusty dagger the Quarg drew a simple map on the ground.

Burstis used the time pondering the same thing that he had spent every day since leaving the town; what had gone wrong with his assassination attempt on Gran in Vicksville? The men he had hired were cutthroats, he certainly knew the type, and had shown no hesitation or remorse in accepting a job to murder a defenseless old woman. When Burstis had seen Gran himself the next day he had at first assumed the men had just failed or gotten too drunk on his money to do the job. A quick visit to their barrel-home had told the true story; they had been killed.

And not in their sleep either, as was being told about the inns of Vicksville. Burstis found it impossible to find tracks in the frozen earth of the alley and too many people had passed through the area for him to readily identify the scent of the killer but he found enough evidence to prove, at least to himself, that the men had been killed but not murdered. Whoever had killed the men had fought them and inflicted a dozen minor wounds on the killers before they died. The slit throats had been an afterthought; not enough blood to have been the cause of death, and that made Burstis very suspicious. Whatever person or persons had killed the two had done it slowly for a reason. The Were could think of two; a personal grudge or someone needing information.

"We are here, and they are here," the Quarg explained, also adding in the rough locations of the human town and one particularly tall hill he called 'the fuzzy one' because of the fog that rose off it at the appropriate time of the year.

"There is a trail that goes here," he added, drawing a serpentine track moving away from the town and off the edge of his map. "Here the trail crosses a little river with high banks. Trees cleared away maybe two of two's years ago for house but we kill that human right after." The Quarg was obviously pleased that he managed to work his advanced mathematics skills into the conversation once again.

"With no trees and the high banks, we'll have cover and they won't. We can probably kill the lot with a single attack," he finished, patting the quiver of arrows on his hip meaningfully.

Burstis considered his options and decided to accept the fellow's suggestion.

"Fine, I'll need to see the place before we're certain; can we get there enough ahead of them to be ready for their arrival?"

Scratching himself the Quarg nodded. "Yeah, no problem. We cut through here and follow the river. It goes straight where trails don't. We get there late tonight; they show up at best the day after. If they know the water is there, they might hurry and try to camp there tomorrow night. Either way we be ready."

Burstis smiled. He had taken on his human form for this discussion and was wearing the untreated furs the Quargs had taken while hunting to ward off the chill. They stank horribly but again he had been forced to leave his clothes behind when he left Vicksville; Weres simply didn't need them and had no ready way to carry them. He dreaded the pain of another change so soon but looked forward to being back in his warm wolf-form.

"All right," he decided, pointing to the place of the proposed ambush. "Bring your warriors in tight and the wolves as well. No one hunts or strays from the main pack as we travel; I don't want someone being discovered by the people we're tracking; they might run the other direction. Get us to this place as quickly as you can so I can look it over. Tell your people that if anyone leaves a single track where it can be seen I'll kill him myself. Do you understand?"

The Quarg leader's eyes narrowed at the threat but he knew better than to complain. With a short nod he rose from his crouch and left the Were to recall his outer ring of scouts.

The Quarg couldn't help considering his situation. Being discovered by the Were and being ordered to help in the ambush was extremely poor timing. Perhaps if they were lucky the Were would leave them after the ambush so they could get back to their scouting mission. To delay now would also delay the intended attack on the human town, and the Quargs were all jealous of the loot their brethren had taken in the sacking of the king's palace. Not a day went by that a few deserters didn't wander through, showing off the gold and silver they had stolen and bragging of all that they had been unable to carry.

If the Were delayed them to the point that they missed out on the sacking of the village the Quarg knew that his days in leading this band might quickly end along with his life. His warriors followed him because of his successes and ambushing a handful of humans in the forest and missing out on the treasures of a whole town would not increase his support. His warriors were not happy with the situation and he was not happy with it, but the pressure of the Were's eyes on his back kept them in line for now. The Quargs to a man had already agreed to flee the situation as soon as it was safe to do so.

But the Quargs had no idea that there was more than one outsider watching them. Well up in a tree, in a spot most people would never look, a hunter watched them all with keen interest.

# Chapter Twenty-One

Using a packhorse to carry your extra food and water invariably sped up a group of travelers as it reduced the loads they had to carry themselves. In most situations that was true, but Gran quickly realized that the packhorse they had could not even keep up with her limping pace.

"Hurry up or I'll make soap out of you," she snarled, having already used up all her best threats long before this. She prodded the poor beast in the backside with her walking stick but saw little result from her efforts; her heart just wasn't in it; the poor thing was obviously doing all that it could.

The Viscount of Gelbow was complaining again. "Gran my feet hurt, can't I ride the horse for a while," he whined.

"You'll kill it," Gran scoffed, shifting the aim of her stick from the horse to the man and giving him a much harder thrust in the identical location. "We're already carrying half its load as it is."

Jamus grumbled some more but mostly just for appearance sake. Despite his best efforts he was slowly getting into better shape from his exertions of the last weeks. The first few days after leaving Vicksville had been most strenuous but he was beginning to become accustomed to walking all day; not that he would ever admit it; he had a reputation to maintain.

Tomo broke up Jamus' ritual complaints when the woodsman came into sight, sitting on his pack on the trail ahead. Gran called a halt when they reached him; the packhorse staggering to one side as it gratefully stopped.

"See anything?" she asked, leaning on her walking stick and thrusting her face almost into Tomo's.

"Not really Gran, just enough to make me suspicious."

"Suspicious of what?" Jamus asked. "Isn't seeing nothing a good thing?"

Tomo shook his head. "Not here, not now. Snow is falling almost every day but not yet accumulating, so the larger animals should be out trying to forage for a few last meals before winter really sets in. I've seen nothing, not even fresh tracks, and that makes me wonder."

"The Were?" Gran whispered.

"Could be, but not alone. One carnivore, not even a Were, could frighten all the game from an area as large as I've covered; not in only a few days. It would take a lot of hunters or a lot more time to kill off or drive away that many animals."

"So we're being watched?" Jamus asked, looking back the way they had come.

"I'm not sure; I haven't seen any tracks of game but I've also not found any sign of large carnivores. Perhaps something moved through here a while back, or is just entering the area now."

"Could it be following us?"

"Not likely, I've been pretty careful about covering our tracks and watching for anything along our back trail," Tomo explained. "If there's anything behind us it's just following the same trail we are, not following us. And it's more than a day behind if then. The trail ahead seems clear as well and I've scouted for some distance in every direction and found nothing. Gran I'm worried."

Gran straightened as far as her bent back would allow. "Humph, you've got nothing to be worried about boy, like as not. There's none better than you in the woods and we know it, like as not."

"Gran I'm good, but I'm not the best, and we both know it. We left a better woodsman back in Vicksville. And even if I were there are times when even the best get surprised; tracking and scouting are not a perfect process."

"You'll do, Tomo, and I'll not hear another word against it," Gran scoffed, grabbing the woodsman's ear and urging him to his feet. "If there's someone or something out there we'll deal with it and to their detriment, like as not."

Unsure what 'detriment' meant Tomo decided to take it as a good thing. "Yes Gran," he intoned, just like he had as a young child. He fell in beside Jamus before he recalled something else.

"Oh, and Gran? The trail starts going down pretty steeply ahead, and as it is a game trail it probably means water. Do you want to keep moving until we get there or stop for the night first?"

"How much water do we have?" she asked.

Jamus reached back to a series of dried gourds hanging from the packhorse. Picking them up by the rawhide strings that held them in place, he shook them to produce a faint gurgling splash.

"Enough for one night," he said, glancing at Tomo for confirmation.

"It won't be the best tasting water ever," nodded the woodsman. "But there's enough for us and the horse."

Gran patted the nose of the animal. "We'd better stop then. Fresh water would be better and the fates know I need to make as much time as possible but we'll just have to camp somewhere and let this poor beast rest."

"Yeah, or we'll be carrying it," mumbled Tomo.

"Sorry, it was the best I could do," argued Jamus. The two had been bickering about the beast since they left Vicksville.

"Enough about the horse," Gran ordered, and the two men complied.

They camped soon after in a small meadow they found near the trail. Tomo cut away some branches from a deadfall and wound them in an out of the remaining branches of a low growing cedar to create a shelter large enough for the three of them. Next he dug down into the frozen dirt and surrounded the hole with flat rocks before building a fire in the pit. The first few times he had done something similar Jamus had been all questions but now understand a little of what the woodsman did; the hole hid the fire while the rocks were used as reflectors to direct the heat into the shelter. The branches around them acted as roof and windbreak while also dissipating the smoke.

Once the horse was unloaded, firewood was obtained, and Gran was busy creating a simple meal the two men stripped the horse and rubbed it down. While Jamus fed and watered the animal Tomo returned to the trail and did what he could to conceal their passage; not too difficult a task with the ground frozen but he did remove a few freshly broken sticks and carefully sprinkled some fallen leaves in places so that they looked to have been undisturbed since they fell.

Once he was finished Tomo was satisfied that anyone passing along the trail would be unlikely to know that they weren't the first travelers to pass this way since winter began. He had done a good job at disguising their trail and their camp, and the watcher was duly impressed. However the watcher knew exactly where the camp was and how many were there; he had been following Tomo all day.

# Chapter Twenty-Two

Two streets over a chandler's shop was burning and nervous homeowners all around were on top of their property with buckets and wet blankets to douse any embers that floated in on the frigid night breeze. The thick smoke drifted up at a slight angle and the smell drove people from the buildings that lay downwind. To the horrified chandler and his family it was a tragedy, to the drunken mercenaries that started it out of spite it was a comedy. And to those hiding in the alley two streets over it was opportunity.

Aldrigal City was under martial law and anyone caught outside after dark was considered to be a criminal or an insurgent. Individuals had been caught and hung from trees and lampposts every night since the city had fallen to the Firthian invaders. Usually younger people and mostly men, those clustered in the alley this night fit nearly all the stereotypes; they were mostly men and definitely insurgents; they were also most certainly criminals.

Hoods had been made of flour sacks to conceal their identities and their clothing was as nondescript as any found in the city. The holes cut to see through were rarely the same size and tended to move about and obscured the vision of the wearers almost as efficiently as it hid their identities. They tended to travel in groups of three or four; looking for one or two Firthians, preferably drunk, to visit their wrath upon. Criminals they might be but they were Aldrigalians too, and Aldrigal had ever resisted invasions. Already the fame of the 'Jackdogs' was being spoken of throughout the city; the insurgents being given the name of the city's fabled defender by a sympathetic public. They accepted it gladly and did what they could to perpetuate the rumors that the Jackdog himself had come to life and led them in their defense.

Eventually the mercenaries grew tired of laughing at the chandler's plight and begin to drift away. Most left together, mindful of the warnings they had received from their commanders about the fates of lone troops in the warrens of this maze-like city. Two, however, younger and braver than the others, and likely more stupid and drunker as well, staggered off together in search of more entertainment. The one detailed to watch them left the shadows and ran down the alleys to where the rest of the group waited and told them of what he had seen. The men in the flour sacks chose to follow the two.

They waited until the mercenaries left the main thoroughfare and crossed through a district of homes before they closed the gap. The area had no lights; those who lived there were too poor to keep lanterns or candles burning overnight, so it was just the sort of place the Jackdogs wanted. It also made for a perfect short cut to the street where most of the city's late night entertainment were located, and saved a traveler several blocks of walking. It was dark, it was quiet, and there were no witnesses. Therefore the two mercenaries died unseen and unheard.

Their nightly deed accomplished the criminals split up after a quick sketch of the Jackdog was drawn on the ground near the bodies, hid their masks, and retreated to a place of hopeful safety. Forced to follow the streets since the rooftops were routinely watched, the insurgents moved from shadow to shadow along the backstreets. Several of their number had been caught and represented some of those being hung for breaking curfew, but this evening the four people from the alley all made it safely to their homes.

Just after dawn a squad of Firthian regulars quick-marched their way from their barracks, through the Merchant's Quarter and out the Merchant's Gate. The buildings there were a uniform two levels in height, each of the structures sharing walls with their neighbors; and were narrow and made of mud brick with a single narrow door and one window directly above it. A few were shops below and homes above but most were divided into smaller one room dwellings accessed by ladders or barrels piled up as steps. The buildings shared a common sense of poverty. Eventually the homes ended on one side of the street and were replaced by a simple plank fence. Above this fence loomed a much larger structure; an inn that had stood there for longer than anyone could remember. It was the inn known as the Jackdog.

A simple gate in the fence allowed the soldiers access into the small courtyard. A pair of large, muscular men left off the wood they were splitting and approached the commander with wide smiles, offering the hospitality of the inn on behalf of their master.

"Your master is here?" the corporal demanded, the glint in his eyes warning the men that no familiarity would be tolerated.

"Of course, I'll get him," one of the men said, smiling and turning away. The other man stood silently, his smile still in place as if no tension was present though he still carried a maul. The corporal scowled at the inn, trying to ignore the grinning jackanapes and so was slow to notice another pair of men emerge from the stables. A glint of sunlight off metal told him of the presence of at least one other on the roof of the inn. It all seemed innocent, but he had his suspicions.

Finally the owner arrived, his smile as large and broad as the others had been. He was very tall man, thin, and had a head of red hair that seemed to deny any attempts at combing. Coming down the steps with hand extended, the man tried to grasp that of the corporal.

Ignoring the hand the soldier spoke.

"Your name is Kelendle? You are the owner of this place?"

"I am, sir," Kelendle agreed, his smile still large as he dropped his hand. "May I offer my hospitality to you and your men?"

Again the corporal ignored the man's words. Turning to the waiting soldiers he barked an order. Immediately four of them stepped forward, producing shackles that were efficiently attached to the innkeeper's wrists and feet. Only the corporal noticed the look the man gave to the gathered wood choppers and stable workers, warning them not to interfere.

"What is the meaning of this?" Kelendle demanded, a look of surprised outrage crossing his face. His face was turning as red as his hair and his hands shook with suppressed anger. The corporal decided that the man was either innocent of any wrong doing or a very accomplished actor. Either way it was not his problem; he only had to bring the man in for questioning. Raising his voice the innkeeper continued to protest his innocence and demanded to know what he was being arrested for.

The commoners gathered by the gate to watch the proceedings all looked shocked and angry and the corporal was glad that he had ordered two of the squad detailed to watch for any possible interference from that direction; this Kelendle was said to be popular among the populace. Once the tall man had been pushed into the center of their formation, his protests ignored by them all, the corporal led the way back through the gate and towards the city guard's former barracks.

Forced to march more slowly to accommodate Kelendle's shackled feet, the soldiers were treated to a constant barrage of spoiled produce and shouted insults from the buildings and crowds they passed. Inside the corporal raged at the insult but he didn't have the time, or the men, to do anything about it now. Later would have to be soon enough; he'd see to it that the people of this street paid for what they were doing. For now, however, he'd have to content himself with helping to interrogate the innkeeper. Hopefully the man would be reluctant to answer questions and force would be necessary to gain his cooperation. The corporal was going to enjoy that.

# Chapter Twenty-Three

"Are your warriors in place, Boz?"

The Quarg looked uncomfortable at Burstis' question but after a quick glance away squared his shoulders and faced the Were. He didn't notice that the Were had remembered his name for the first time.

"Yes, I sent them into the trees hours ago, but three were missing; they didn't come back from gathering wood this morning. They must have deserted." The Quarg didn't even look proud of now knowing the much larger number of 'three', taught him by the Were.

Baffled, Burstis stammered, "Why?"

Shrugging the Quarg looked and sounded as confused as the Were. "I'm not sure. They either went after the main host for a greater chance at plunder or went home."

Pursing his lips, Burstis took a moment to think. He still had enough warriors to do the job but Quargs brave enough to flee a Were was troubling.

"What of your wolves?"

"They are there, in the woods behind us. It was the only way I could keep them from attacking at first scent of the humans. When I whistle, they'll come running."

Burstis paused only a second before speaking again. "We finish the ambush and kill the old woman. After that we deal with these cowards. I'll wait here to see that you take the humans. If your rogue Were shows himself, I'll handle him."

Nodding once in agreement the Quarg turned and made his way down the riverbank in a crouch to keep out of sight. No bridge had ever been built but the river rarely ran deep enough to have made one convenient. The edges of the flow had already frozen thickly enough to walk on and only the very center of the current flowed freely. He had warriors in the woods to both sides of the trail and more hidden here below the steep banks of the river. Others would come up behind the humans and drive them into the ambush and two were in the ruins of the house that sat in the middle of the clearing just in case their prey tried to take cover within. Twenty archers, or as the Quarg thought of it four full hands worth, were enough to kill three humans. Only the rogue Were concerned him and Lord Burstis seemed more than fit to handle the one-armed beast. Boz didn't know that the warriors he had ordered to his left flank were no longer there.

Moving down the riverbank Boz checked with those warriors. They had bows in their hands and spears leaning nearby; ready to participate in the kill in mid-field or close to fight hand to hand if the humans somehow survived the initial barrage and ran for the river. They seemed to be in high spirits and looking forward to the kill; none of them had any ideas as to why the others had deserted.

"Staz was a coward and Logg do what Staz say," was all they had to share. Boz knew them all well; they weren't lying to him. Whatever the reason for the desertion they hadn't shared their concerns with the others before they left.

A horn sounded in the woods back up the trail; the trailing Quargs had been seen and were actively driving the humans towards the river. Those in the ambush made no sound of acknowledgement, but Boz watched as those by the riverbank placed arrows to strings and waited for the signal. Just before the humans broke free from the trees those in pursuit would sound their horns again and everyone would attack. It should be a quick, easy slaughter; a couple of arrows apiece and a few throats to slit and it should be done. Time seemed to crawl as the warriors excitedly waited; the humans must be moving very slowly, perhaps pausing to exchange arrows with their pursuers or trying to flee in another direction. Boz kept the heads of his warriors down despite the longer than expected wait; the humans had to come this way; the terrain and pursuing Quargs made that a certainty. Finally, just as Boz himself was about to risk a quick peek over the riverbank, the horn sounded again. Much closer this time; the ambush was sprung.

Springing to their feet the Quargs in the riverbed screamed their war cries as they launched their first volley of arrows towards the trail. As planned they grabbed up their spears and climbed to the top of the bank and made ready to cut off any survivors if they ran towards the river. Surprised the Quargs stopped in mid-yell, seeing no sign of the humans anywhere.

Two Quarg heads emerged from the ruined home; a simple structure built of logs and now without a roof, and looked about uneasily as four more warriors slowly came from the woods to Boz's right. Of the pursuing band nothing was seen, nor from the warriors stationed to the left.

Giving a low-pitched whistle Boz motioned for the Quarg furthest from him to move into the woods and scout about. Next he caught the eye of one of the warriors in the house and motioned him to check on the woods to his left. Making a rude gesture the Quarg from the house refused the request and disappeared back inside.

Growling to himself Boz made a mental note to punish the warrior but knew that it would have to wait; where was everyone? The trail was empty and over half of his Quargs had not responded to the second horn blast. Turning to look upstream Boz searched out the waiting Burstis and gave the Were an exaggerated shrug; he certainly did not know what was going on. His thoughts were interrupted by a scream.

"Over there," growled the next Quarg, pointing towards the woods where the scout had disappeared a moment before. Following the jutting of his chin the Quarg pulled the string of his bow back and fired randomly in that direction, his missile striking a poplar well above the ground.

"Stop wasting arrows, fool," Boz growled, giving he fellow a cuff. "Keep an eye on those woods and choose your target."

Just then Boz saw a flash of brown up the trail. He hadn't been looking directly at it but detected the movement from the corner of his eye. The color was a mere impression but he was hopeful it was the hides worn by one of his men. Taking a step that direction he peered hard but saw nothing more; there were no Quargs coming.

A grunt of pain was followed by a gurgling scream as another of the Quargs nearest the wood line died; the arrow through his throat drowning him in his own blood even as he fell. Boz turned and dived back beneath the cover of the riverbank, shouting for his remaining warriors to do the same though most of them beat him to the shelter. Boz watched as his remaining warriors ran; even those in the house vacating it to join their fellows. Another arrow emerged from the trees, striking the ground near the foot of a running Quarg, then another skipped off of a rock near the riverbank, but the remaining warriors reached safety without injury. Hurriedly Boz tried to count how many were with him, and finally decided that if you took away one finger from each hand he had two hands of warriors. Holding up those eight fingers he turned to show them to Burstis only to discover that the Were was gone now too.

"Eeeee! Eeeee!" squealed one of the Quargs, the warrior sitting on the frozen ground clutching his knees was the same one who had refused Boz's order before. Obgog was not the mightiest of warriors but his panic was frightening the others more than they already were. Stepping over to Obgog Boz slapped the fellow hard across the cheek.

"Pull yourself together 'Gog, we're in a fight here."

"Arrows from the trees! It's the Keon-din," wailed Obgog.

"The Keon-din is dead," growled a nearby warrior. "Tigdut's band saw him die on the road weeks ago; he had a dozen arrows through his brisket."

"He's not dead but he's sure not around here," argued another. "He can't die but he can't live outside his home forest; he's a spirit cursed to haunt that area forever."

Boz cursed them both. "It's not the Keon-din; I've seen the arrows used by the demon and these are not his," he explained, snatching up the arrow that had struck the rock and fallen harmlessly to the ice of the river. It was a well made arrow but did not carry the distinctive colors the Keon-din used; the three black stripes just behind the arrowhead were missing.

"That don't mean nothing," sneered the first warrior.

"I don't care who it is; Keon-din or not I'm getting out of here," stated a larger warrior from downstream. "I can't kill what I can't see."

Boz wasn't sure what they should do, but he knew how to handle this problem. Waiting until the larger Quarg was about to pass him, Boz threw a stiff jab that dropped the warrior in his tracks.

"We leave when I saw we leave," he growled, clutching the handle of his knife threateningly. Thankfully no one else tried to flee and even Obgog seemed to pull himself together somewhat. "If we try to leave now we'll have that Were to deal with; anyone want to be his next meal?"

Gathering themselves the Quargs moved back to the riverbank and studied the trees. After a few moments the warrior he had struck came to and joined them, saying nothing to Boz as he did so.

"Where is that Were?" Obgog asked, his trembling easing. "Did he run off?"

"Nah, the Keon-din ate him," joked Storak. "He'll probably be spitting up fur balls for weeks."

Despite their fear the Quargs all joined in on the laughter, weak though it was. Boz silently thanked the other warrior for his support; Storak didn't speak often but had a way of easing the fears of others when he did.

Other jokes, each more ribald than the last, were passed as the Quargs scanned the forest for any sign of their attackers. Their courage grew as the time passed and soon enough even Obgog was blatantly bragging about 'what he would do' if the Keon-din himself dared to show his face. Laughter rang from the riverbed as their spirits improved, that is until someone noticed that Storak wasn't laughing.

"Hey Storak," joked Obgog, jabbing his friend in the shoulder. "I laughed at your weak joke, surely you can..." his voice trailed away. Storak was dead; an arrow had punched through his forehead and he had died without a sound.

Shocked they stared at the dead Quarg, the silence not broken until another Quarg, a small warrior named Yarp, screamed and fell; yet another arrow jutting through his forearm.

"Where are they coming from?" Boz demanded, trying to look in all directions at once.

"From there," squealed Obgog, back to holding his knees. He was pointing behind them. The riverbank on that side was not as high and the trees were even closer; whoever their enemies were they had a clear shot at the Quargs.

"Into the man-hut," Boz ordered, leading the way up and onto the steep bank and running hard for the log structure. An arrow passed closely to his ear and struck the wall so he didn't bother running around to the door but instead dived headlong through the window. He heard a grunt and then a crash as someone slammed into the doorjamb, then someone else came through the same window he did and landed atop him. Just after that Quarg another came through, and Boz found himself beneath two of his brethren.

Forcing the others off of him Boz began snarling and kicking anyone who came too close as he regained his feet. Snatching up his bow he found it broken, and then realized that all but two of his arrows had fallen from his quiver during his run. Cursing just the way his father had taught him he peered out the window and then ducked away, hearing yet another arrow strike the wall an instant later.

Looking about he found himself to be one of only four Quargs in the house. Obgog had been the first to fall on him and it had been Harket who had nearly broken his shoulder when he collided with the empty doorjamb. Yarp was also there, the arrow still protruding from his forearm.

"Where are the others?" Boz panted, glaring at his remaining men.

"Waxis ran upstream," panted Harket. "And Igar is dead."

"Dead or wounded?" Boz demanded. "Where is he?"

"Right out there," Harket pointed. Igar was indeed laying just outside the door of the house, dead with an arrow through his chest. It took Boz a moment to realize what exactly was wrong but eventually it came to him.

"That arrow came from the other direction." He growled. He had assumed that their attackers had crossed the river up or downstream and attacked from behind; now it appeared that there were more enemies than he had been told.

"Ospat is alive but he's wounded," stated Yarp, grimacing through the pain. "An arrow took him in the leg as we were running."

Risking another glance back towards the river Boz did indeed see Ospat squirming about in the dirt; the pain must be incredible to keep him from playing dead.

"What of Axblit, anyone see what happened to him?" asked Boz as another arrow ricocheted off the window frame and then bounced harmlessly from the opposite wall.

The Quargs looked at one another, and then shook their heads. No one had seen anything.

"We gotta make a break for it, Boz," stated Harket. "The woods are close, we get there we just keep on running."

"And how many die getting there?" whined Obgog.

"More will die if we stay here."

"What about the wolves?" demanded Yarp. "Whistle for them and they'll keep those humans busy; might even kill them for us."

"Yeah, whistle up the wolves, Boz," agreed Obgog.

Realizing that the wolves were their best hope, Boz gave his most piercing, distance-carrying whistle without voicing his fears that the wolves may have been removed already. The second wave of arrows had come from roughly the same location as the wolves had been left. What could kill a dozen wolves without any sound? Trying to measure time Boz counted his heartbeats all the way to three once for each finger and toe he had before whistling again. By the time he whistled for the third time they all knew that the wolves were not coming.

"Now what do we do?" Obgog demanded, tears flowing down his cheeks. "We're gonna die here."

"No we're not," stated Boz, kicking the smaller Quarg for emphasis. "That Were is still out there and he needs us; he won't be afraid of no arrows; all we have to do is sit still and he'll come for us when he's dealt with whoever is shooting at us."

"It's the Keon-din, it has to be," sobbed Obgog.

"It's those humans," Boz replied, considering kicking the Quarg again but decided against it. "There were two men; one is behind us and one ahead. That's all it is."

"Then where are the others? There were five Quargs behind them, and four more over there," Harket said, pointing to what had originally been the left flank of the ambush. "Not to mention Jubsput with the wolves."

"And the three that ran off last night," added Yarp. "I don't think they ran anywhere."

"That's enough of that," Boz ordered, turning to stare each Quarg in the eye. "We stay here until the Were does something, then we make a break for it. We stay together after we reach the trees. If we see a human, we kill him. Now everyone get ready to move."

Reluctantly they gathered together what weapons they still had, only Harket had a working bow so they gave their arrows to him, and gathered together in a crouch by the door listening for something, anything, that might mean that it was safe for them to emerge. Hours passed as they waited, the time broken only by an occasional arrow striking a log. Yarp was beginning to look bad; his skin was pale from the loss of blood yet still they waited for a sign, for something. Finally, it came.

The howl of the Were was obviously not that of a wolf. It was too loud, too powerful, and was not the long, undulating howl of a mere animal. The cry was strong, victorious, and indicated that the Were had both fought and won.

Urging his remaining warriors to their feet Boz led them out of the house and across the clearing.

# Chapter Twenty-Four

"It just doesn't feel right, Gran," Tomo said as he studied the earth. The poacher turned woodsman was on his knees in the midst of the trail; worriedly examining the others knew not what.

"This trail is here because it leads to water; that's why the animals made it. Someone else, a farmer perhaps, widened it at one point for wagons but that was only temporary," he explained, pointing to a sapling growing nearby. "You can see that the undergrowth has grown back."

"So the trail was abandoned," offered Jamus. "What doesn't feel right?"

Lowering his face nearly to the ground Tomo replied, "the lack of animals, the lack of sign, along this trail. The animals have used this same path for years, maybe centuries. After the trail was abandoned by man, they began using it again. Now I see no sign of passage for at least three days. Why?"

Gran remained silent, staring at the packed and frozen dirt as if demanding it to give her an answer. The nobleman was certain that he had no idea what the other man was talking about but he continued to ask questions, hoping that answering would help Tomo figure out the problem.

"You've said yourself that the ground is too frozen to leave tracks," he said. "Why does it seem odd to you that there are none?"

Tomo nodded once as if the question was a good one then waved for Jamus to follow him off the trail. "See here, where the snow didn't melt back under the trees? Those tracks belong to a puma, or another big cat. They approach the trail here," he pointed, "then as he gets close he suddenly turns and runs away. Why? And tracks aren't the only sign left by animals; there are no broken sticks, no nail marks in the dirt, no bent or broken branches on the brush; animals leave less sign than humans do, but they do leave something. Particularly the larger ones. A bear doesn't care if he breaks off a branch or two, and I've seen nothing to indicate that any creatures are using this trail."

"Their water is dry?"

"Nope, its snowed too much lately and most of it has melted. Wrong time of year for it to be that dry and we haven't had a drought around here in ten years or more. They're obviously getting their water somewhere else but the question is, why abandon this trail?"

"So what do we do, Tomo?" asked Gran, speaking unexpectedly.

"I'd like to leave the trail, Gran, but that makes for hard travel, and I don't know this area like I do back home. We won't get lost, but climbing some of these hills will be tough on... the horse," Tomo replied, only narrowly avoiding saying that it was Gran he was worried about. The horse wouldn't live out the winter in any event.

"Do you think there's someone ahead of us or behind?"

"I can't be sure Gran, it just as easily could be both."

Jamus began to get nervous. "So are we talking Quargs, wolves, Weres, or humans from Vicksville?"

"Again, it could be all of those. Gran is wanted, it may be that she was recognized; you remember those men that came in the hospital that night? They might have followed us, or anyone that wanted the reward. You already know about the others."

Patting Tomo's head Gran mumbled that he was 'a good boy' and then began to pace, her walking stick making faint taps on the hard ground as she traveled in a circle without leaving the path. Already her limp was nearly gone, and both men had a moment to wonder about the healing ability of the woman. After her third lap she seemed to come to a decision.

"If it were Quargs and wolves, where would they attack us?"

Thinking for a moment, Tomo replied. "If they were on their own, as soon as they caught wind of us. They're not much for patience, not when they're out looking for trouble to begin with. Three humans wouldn't represent much of a threat, and the packhorse would make them greedy."

"And if they were led by a Were?"

Looking decidedly unhappy at the thought he said, "Then he'd use his brain, if he could, and organize an ambush somewhere; probably where the trail passes below a cliff or through an open field maybe. Or somewhere we would be separated."

"But leaving the trail would slow us down? We need speed, Tomo."

"Yes Gran, I understand, but better slow than dead. If they're planning an ambush, it won't be behind us and likely won't be too far ahead, either. We might already be within their control."

Gran stared ahead, seeing nothing as the trail angled steadily downward until it disappeared from view.

"How far to the water?" she asked.

Using a shrug as his answer, Tomo remained quiet.

Thumping both men once with her staff, Gran ordered them on. "We'll stay with the trail until we get beyond that ditch of brambles, then we'll leave the trail and make for Skallist," she declared.

"Ok, Gran, but let me scout that ditch first; that's a good place for an ambush right there."

Tomo carefully and alertly walked down to the ditch, ready to dive for cover at the first hint of movement. Finding nothing there he had just begun the walk back up the hill when he saw movement on the trail behind his friends.

The wail of a Quarg war horn drowned out his shout of warning but Gran and Jamus got the message. Leaping forward Jamus covered half the distance to Tomo before he thought to look back for Gran. The old woman was tugging on the horse's halter as the feeble beast tried to keep up.

Slipping as he turned Jamus almost fell. Running back to Gran he slapped the halter from her hand and unceremoniously scooped the woman up over his shoulders. Running again towards Tomo, trying to ignore the screeching and wailing of his passenger as she detailed the beatings he would suffer for carrying her like a sack of cabbages, the nobleman passed the woodsman and leaped across the ditch on the run. Pausing only to launch an arrow at the descending Quargs, Tomo followed in the viscount's wake and quickly pulled even.

"Gotta... leave... the trail..." Tomo gasped, angling to his left to lead the way. Jamus merely grunted but followed, Gran's screams were now curses intended for the Quargs. Just as he left the trail, something caught Tomo's eye, and he immediately shifted direction and shoulder-blocked Jamus ahead of him in the other direction. Still leaving the trail, they were now running to the right of it.

Moving to cut them off the Quargs began hooting at them, calling in their own language for the humans to stand and fight. Each of the humanoids carried bows but they didn't fire; the branches and tree trunks, not to mention their momentum and that of their prey, would have made the shot impossible. Despite his fear, and the necessity of watching his feet to avoid brambles, fallen branches, and depressions in the ground that might trip him, Tomo noticed that the Quargs were running much faster than the humans were, but seemed more intent on cutting them off from their chosen direction than catching them.

"That tree," he panted, slapping Jamus on the shoulder to get his attention. Stumbling, already tired, the two changed directions slightly again and ran towards the remains of a log that must have once been the pride of the forest. It was massive and even on its side and partially buried in the ground it stood as tall as either man. With pausing Tomo scrambled up the side, then reached back to help Gran off of Jamus' shoulder. The Quarg's shouts turned to anger as they also stopped and began loading their bows. Clutching Jamus' hand Tomo pulled him up, with all three rolling onto the cold ground in a less than dignified pile just as the Quarg arrows struck the tree.

Crouching down the three worked to regain their breaths, Gran all the while whipping Jamus with her switch despite not having the strength to make him feel it. Tomo slid an arrow onto his bow and tried to listen over the gasps for air for the sounds of an approaching Quarg.

"Why did you change your mind back there," Jamus finally gasped. "I almost fell."

Tomo, his breath the first to slow, took a quick peek over the log before he replied. "I saw a sign on the trail; an old woodsman's sign that said to come this way."

"I didn't see a sign."

"It was there, in the middle of the trail; two rocks piled atop each other with a third one on this side. Trust me; we were supposed to go this way."

"A sign from who?" Jamus said incredulously, his breathing finally slowing as well. "It could have been the Quargs that put that sign there."

"Hush now, Tomo knows what he's doing," Gran said, her sides still heaving but she put the switch away.

"Watch that way, Gran, and you this way Jamus. If you see a Quarg trying to work his way around us to get a clear shot, let me know," Tomo ordered, standing back up to peek over the log again. Another arrow struck the tree as he appeared; the timing had been perfect if the missile had been better aimed. Turning to the others Tomo opened his mouth just as a cry of pain sounded from uphill.

"I see one," Gran croaked, her voice breaking but her hand steady as she pointed back in the direction of the trail. A flash of movement was all Jamus saw when he looked.

"A Quarg?"

"Well it wasn't the Aldrigalian House Guards," she snarled, banging her walking staff lightly into the nobleman's forehead.

"Switch with me, Jamus. Gran you take Jamus' side," Tomo stated, dropping to a knee and drawing back on his bow.

The others obediently accepted their new tasks; Gran looking the other direction and Jamus tiptoeing to look over the tree, but they keep the corner of their eyes on the woodsman. Carefully Tomo took aim, at what the others couldn't see even when they peeked, and held his bow fully drawn. Time passed slowly, the silence broken only by a grunt from uphill likely meant to keep them looking that direction, and Tomo's arm began to shiver. He lowered the weapon for a moment to rest it, then redrew the bow and resumed his aim. Then, so suddenly Jamus gasped in surprise, Tomo released the arrow to fly into the lower limbs of a low-growing evergreen, causing the tree to emit a high-pitched shriek.

"Didn't kill him, but he won't be too mobile," Tomo grinned, looking over his shoulder to meet the eyes of a smiling Jamus. Neither man noticed the shadow that fell across Gran, nor the towering figure that cast it from his position atop the log.

# Chapter Twenty-Five

Justice Square was the official name for the home compound of the Aldrigal City Watch. Locals called it by a variety of names depending on whether or not they occasionally bent, or broke entirely, local ordinances. Mostly it was called, simply, 'the hole'.

There were no defensive works; no walls, no towers; just a series of buildings and one open area where the prisoners were housed. The barracks sat on the east side of the plaza and were normally the home of the younger, unmarried members of the watch. These days it was two squads of the Second Firthian Light Foot who lived there. To the north side of the square was the Justiciary, a massive building of cut stone that held courtrooms. Behind those were the homes of the adjudicators that heard the cases brought before them by the City Watch members. West of the square was the buildings where the city officials pushed their parchments about and passed laws to punish the peasantry and irritate the nobility. Southward lay the only street that accessed the square and it was lined with businesses that catered to the Watch or its prisoners. In the very center of the plaza was the hole.

Decades before a prison had stood here; complete with cells and dungeons and other appropriate paraphernalia. The original building had burned and later collapsed when a sinkhole opened up beneath the ruins. When the wreckage had been cleared away the city officials found themselves unwilling to spend the coin necessary to rebuild so they instead refurbished the hole itself, installing cells around the perimeter and leaving the central portion of the hole open to the sky.

The cells themselves were small, dank and rarely used, and located against the walls of the roughly circular room at the bottom of the hole. Most prisoners were lowered into the pit and allowed to roam about freely, choosing a blanket from among the lice-ridden pile left there and finding a place on the stone floor beneath the overhang that fronted the cells. There was plenty of room for them under the overhang in most cases, as prisoners were usually not there for long. These days, however, every inch of floor was full.

"I'm not even from Aldrigal," whined a fat elven merchant as he shivered in the very center of hole. Today that was the best place to be, as the feeble rays of the sun struck only that spot for but a short time each day. He'd nearly emptied his purse to pay some of his larger prisoners to claim it for him.

"Shut up!" came the chorus from the gathered prisoners. To a man they were sick of the elf's complaints.

Trembling the man tried to keep quiet but his nature took over again. "Why won't they throw down some more firewood?"

"I wish they would, just so it would land on your head," shouted a prisoner.

Kelendle was sitting near the elf and decided to have some mercy on his fellows and engage the man in conversation; anything to keep him from complaining out loud.

"Listen, friend, your complaining is just going to get you beaten again; everyone here is suffering the same as you are," he said, keeping his voice low in the hopes that any replies would return in the same tone.

"But I don't belong here, I've done nothing," he whined, again repeating himself. "I'm not even from Aldrigal; I was just passing through!"

Nudging the elf Kelendle caught the man's eye and spoke softly again. "Most of the people down here did nothing wrong; they're just suspected of it. Until the Firthians feel that they have pacified the city they'll keep throwing people in here just on suspicion. That's why I'm here; they suspect that I'm in the resistance."

"But why do we have to be in this hole? What if it rains?"

"If it rains, we'll get wet. There's a drain around here someplace but it's mostly stopped up. Prisoners down here in the spring have to sleep sitting up to keep from drowning. The snow is bad enough; but see those pipes up there?" Kelendle pointed upwards. Halfway up the shaft a series of small pipes, none larger than a man's fist, thrust out from the stone.

"Yes."

"Those are sewer pipes that drain the water runoff from this whole section of the city. It all empties in here and, eventually, runs out through the drain and into the river. The drain itself is the same size as those pipes up there."

Looking even more miserable than ever the elf cut his eyes at Kelendle. "Why are you telling me all this?"

"Just to let you know that as bad as it is right now, it can and will get worse. 'Once you know what's coming, you might be able to tolerate what you have a little more.'"

A feeble smile pulled up the corners of the elf's mouth. "That's a Jackdog quote. I remember that story."

"'The Jackdog and the Jailers Wife,' has always been one of my favorites," Kelendle explained. "And that is precisely why the Firthians believe that I'm a member of the resistance."

Confused the merchant asked, "Because you like old fables?"

"No, because the resistance has been named 'the Jackdogs' by the citizens, and my inn is named the 'Jackdog'.

"That's a pretty far stretch."

"Yes it is, yet here I sit in the same position as you. Yet I have not been beaten once for complaining. Think on it, friend."

"Kelendle, the boss wants to talk to you," came a rough voice from behind them. Turning the innkeeper recognized a thug from one of the street gangs. The man did not look like he was making a request.

Excusing himself Kelendle stood stiffly to his feet, gathered his ratty blanket about his narrow shoulders and followed the man through the crowd. Easily the tallest man in the hole, he could see to every part of the place even when everyone was standing. Their destination was obviously a cell in the northern wall where a number of people he knew were gathered. The various gangs were well represented here and each had claimed a place for themselves. The two largest gangs in Aldrigal City, the Muggers and the Bricklayers, even had their top bosses here and it was towards the Mugger's side of the hole that they were destined.

Some of those sitting around the cells nodded to Kelendle as he passed while others glared or ignored him altogether. Inside the cell the boss of the Muggers, a mean-looking fellow named Kent sat next to the boss of the Bricklayers, a woman named Clowdia. Not known as firm friends it appeared that they had found some common cause here in the hole.

Being intended for only one person the cells were narrow and nearly filled with a single bunk. To speak with any privacy the two bosses were sitting together on the cot and had to squeeze together to allow Kelendle to join them. The three of them filled every inch of the cot but with some of the larger bruisers from each gang sitting just outside the door they could at least enjoy a measure of privacy.

The greetings were quick and terse. "Kelendle we need some information," spoke up Kent immediately. The man normally kept his head shaved but after a week in the hole the stubble was coming in just above his ears. A scar across the top of his head looked bad but no worse than the severe crook to his nose.

"And we don't expect to be charged for it neither," added Clowdia. She was an attractive lady but her life had been tough and she was a reflection of that.

"Common cause, my friends," Kelendle smiled.

"Yeah, well we have a plan to get out of here but we need to know a few things before we try," Kent stated, his voice pitched low. "One is; can we expect any help from the resistance if we do escape? The Firthians will assume we're against them."

Keeping his face impassive Kelendle denied knowing anything about the resistance but added, "I would assume that those patriots would welcome any assistance they could garner against the invaders."

"He means they won't help us unless we actively help the resistance," Clowdia explained.

Kent nodded and continued. "The second is; can you get a message out?"

Clowdia added, "We can get messages in, some of our people have been dropping notes in during the night, but we have no way of getting word back out again."

"Yeah, most of our people are down here," grouched Kent. "And the guards we used to bribe are dead or prisoners too."

"What of those who leave?" Kelendle asked. "A few get taken out every day."

"And those are hung, or so says the word we're getting," Kent replied.

"Here's the deal, Kelendle," Clowdia said as she turned as much as possible to face the taller man. "You get word to your people who will in turn get a hold of whatever people Kent and I still have free and combined all three groups stage an escape; nothing dramatic, just slip in, take out a couple of guards, and drop the ladders down. Once we're free our gangs help the resistance."

"And don't try to claim that you don't have anyone who can handle the breakout," growled Kent. "You got some of the best bully-boys in the city on your payroll."

"What of the Greens? Or the Bag Street Boys?" responded Kelendle. "There are a dozen or more gangs represented down here; have you tried to recruit any of them? And what of Prince Manix?" Kelendle said, waving vaguely towards the cell where the captured prince was kept. "Surely he has some influence?"

Sharing a look the two bosses nodded slightly to one another before Clowdia spoke. "Truth is, we don't trust the other gangs, and not the Greens in particular. We've found a few of the gangs have Firthian gold in their purses. Enough that we don't dare enlist anyone we don't know. If the Prince has any influence it's not apparent; he's still down here just like the rest of us."

Shouts of dismay from the outer room drowned out Kelendle's eventual response, forcing him to repeat it. Apparently more people were being sent down the ladders, ensuring that no one save the bosses in the cells would be able to lie down to sleep.

"I'll see what I can do."

# Chapter Twenty-Six

Being pummeled from three directions Mute tried to his best to block Gran's switch as it stung the most. Thankfully no one's heart was really in it.

"You big oaf! You nearly stopped my heart," Gran yelled as she now plied her switch in earnest. "Scared me out of a year of life, like as not."

Tomo and Jamus were no less upset; each had thought that the Quargs had them when the big man had jumped off the log and into their midst. Mute wasn't making things any better as he smiled and gave his croaking laugh.

"Can't you just grow up?" demanded Gran with a last twitch of her switch. Anyone who knew her could tell that she wasn't upset by the man's arrival.

Mute replied by hand signal; pointing first at Gran and then holding up a single finger.

"You first," she translated, then pulled her switch back out for one last half-hearted swat.

"I figured you were coming," smiled Tomo, returning to watching the direction of his last arrow. "That was your warning on the trail, wasn't it?"

Mute smiled and patted Tomo's head. Tomo gave him a curse. "Stop telling me I'm a 'good boy'."

Holding up a hand Jamus asked Gran, "I thought you said he was still too weak to travel? And what of those men watching him; they were put there by the Mayor to keep him from leaving, weren't they?"

Gran patted Jamus' hand. "Well the answer to your first question is that I lied, and the second is yes, they were."

"Nobody can keep... Mute here, cooped up if he doesn't want to be," Tomo laughed to cover his almost-mistake, then giving Jamus a shove and motioned for him to keep watch. "I imagine he left the night after we did, right?"

Mute nodded, then hugged Gran.

"What about the Quargs?" Jamus asked, nervously scanning the trees in his direction.

Mute jerked a thumb over his shoulder and then drew a finger along his neck. Next he pointed to his right and then his left and held up a single finger each time.

"He says there's one to either side but he took care of the others."

"Well the one on this side shouldn't be a problem anymore," stated Tomo.

Motioning for them to wait Mute climbed over the log and disappeared, leaving them alone for some time as he made a circuit around the area. When he finally returned he stopped well away and banged two sticks together before walking back to join them.

"Smart," commented Tomo to the others as they watched the big woodsman return. "The sticks got our attention but kept us from firing blindly."

"Yeah, I guess he couldn't just shout," Jamus replied.

Flashing his hands in a furious series of movements, Mute explained what he had found as Gran translated.

"The Quarg you hit is dead," she began, adding on her own that Mute probably finished the wounded brute. "The one that circled around that direction ran off, but there are more of them waiting down below to ambush us."

Holding up a hand to forestall Jamus' question she continued. "There are also Weres around, at least one but maybe more. And quite a few wolves but they seem to have wandered away from the Quargs, Mute isn't sure why."

"So what do we do?" Jamus asked.

"How many Quargs are here? And where is the Were?" asked Tomo

Again Gran translated. "The Were moved off to the north, chasing or following the wolves, Mute's not sure which. He's not sure how many Quargs are left, probably at least ten or so. Apparently he's killed a lot of Quargs today already, and the rest are down the trail, waiting to ambush us by a river."

"Then which direction do we go?"

Mute was still making signs so Gran didn't hear Tomo's question. "He says that we should go ahead and trip the trap; turn the ambush back on the Quargs. Teach them mathematics, no, wait, I mean 'teach them a lesson'," Gran said. "Sorry, it's been a while since I learned hand-talk."

"How?"

Mute took something off his shoulder, handing a polished buffalo-horn to Jamus and then pantomiming for him to blow it. Then he dropped to one knee and pretended to fire his bow. Next he pointed at the sun and again at another point in the sky, then looked to Gran.

"He says we set up near where the trail opens up on the river, and then we blow the horn and wait. If we see Quargs, we shoot arrows at them but for us not to leave here for an hour," she translated.

"And what will he be doing?" Jamus asked, noticing the 'we'.

Pointing to the trees Mute pantomimed walking, and then pretended to skulk around as he moved his arm around in a large half circle before patting his bow.

"He's going to circle around, attack from behind, I got it," the viscount said.

Once Mute was gone the others checked themselves over for wounds and then spent the time resting and drank everything in their water bottles. With the river this close they decided not to conserve; they would either have access to it soon or they would be dead if their counter-ambush failed. Once the hour had passed they made their way back to the trail, finding their horse dozing there unharmed, and then made their slow way downhill towards the river through the brush. Some distance back they blew the horn and then left Gran to hold the horse while the two men crept forward on their bellies until they were at the edge of the clearing. A small cabin, nearly collapsed was the only thing they could see. Soon enough Tomo spotted movement along the riverbank itself and pointed it out to Jamus.

Both men loaded their bows and waited. Not for the first time since leaving Vicksville Tomo cursed the poor quality of the arrows bought there by the nobleman. Both he and Mute had agreed that they weren't half what they could make for themselves but there had been little other choice; they hadn't had the time or materials to do so. Time seemed to drag past without sight or sound of the Quargs but finally the silence was broken by a faint spurt of laughter, followed later by a cry of pain. Then the Quargs were coming over the riverbank in a wave; some screaming and others silent, as they charged towards the two humans. Firing as quickly as they could the two men managed to put five arrows into the air, three by Tomo, before the destination of the Quargs became apparent; they were taking shelter in the ruined home. One Quarg at least fell in the charge; dying only an arm-length away form the cabin's door. Other missiles launched from across the river had wounded another but Mute finished him with a second arrow while the men watched.

"How many did you see?" asked Tomo.

"Go in the building? Two, maybe. I'm not sure. What do we do now?"

Having no other ideas they waited, watching the cabin and firing an occasional arrow when a target presented itself. At one point Jamus crawled back to update Gran, but the hours drug by slowly as the two men lay on the icy ground. Both were shivering by the time the long, undulating howl of a wolf sounded in the woods to their right. As if awaiting that signal the Quargs immediately burst from the cabin, rushing headlong towards the direction of the howl. Caught somewhat unawares, the two men barely had time to reach their knees and fire an arrow apiece before the leading Quargs disappeared into the underbrush... only to reappear a second later and run headlong into their fellows.

"Keon-din," one fallen warrior screamed, trying to run while still laying on his stomach. Like actors in a comedic play the fallen Quargs leaped to their feet and ran in all directions as if sense had fled them, making them moving targets but without any cover. Before long three were dead and one had leaped from the riverbank and out of sight.

Mute emerged from the trees and began harvesting every arrow he could find. Even those that were damaged in some way were taken; the points could be reused. Tomo helped him, pausing to dispatch one Quarg that wasn't completely dead as Jamus went back for Gran and the packhorse. By nightfall they had crossed the river, finding the last Quarg unconscious on the ice where he had struck it face first, and were several miles further down the trail. That night they made camp under an overhang of stone and ate cold mutton and dried apples. The conversation was kept low but remained joyous as they discussed the antics of the frightened Quargs.

"How did you howl like that?" Tomo demanded at one point, punching Mute solidly on the shoulder. Smiling the big woodsman reached under his shirt and pulled out a leather bag that hung around his neck on a leather cord. The pouch was small but looked to be stuffed full. Jamus remembered seeing it when caring for the man and thought that it was some sort of good-luck charm.

Opening the top of the pouch Mute shook it upside down until a small tube emerged, dangling loosely from the opening. Taking the tube between two fingers he pulled it taught, it stretched to twice its length, before squeezing the bag lightly. The faint howl of a wolf emerged from tube and undulated as Mute stretched or relaxed the neck.

"It was much louder than that," Tomo protested. Mute replied by pantomime; pretending to squeeze the pouch harder and lifting his hands up into the air.

"You squeeze it harder and it's louder?" Tomo guessed.

"Where did you get that?" Gran demanded.

Another series of hand signals left the two men clueless, but Gran obviously understood.

"Oh, him," she sniffed, dropping the subject and leaving the others in the dark.

Eventually Mute told everyone, through Gran, that he was going to sleep elsewhere, and that he would take care of the watch for the night. Grateful for the extra rest no one argued, and the big woodsman soon disappeared into the darkness alone.

Silence reigned after he left but Jamus finally had to break it.

"Who is he?" he asked, looking from one companion to the other. It was some time before either bothered to reply.

"I told you, Jamus. I knew him as a boy," answered Tomo, his words coming a little too quickly to be the entire truth. "We were friends."

Before the viscount could protest Gran interrupted.

"It's alright Tomo, I think sir high-and-mighty here can be trusted, just so long as he's within my arm's reach, like as not," she said, her glare not having quite the usual bite. Not wanting to break her train of thought, Jamus wisely waited until she broke her own silence.

"Mute is his latest name, but as I'm sure you already know he's had a lot more than one in his life. He was a good boy growing up; the best at everything he turned his hand to."

"Best woodsman I've ever seen," added Tomo.

Ignoring the interruption Gran continued. "He was a wonderful dancer and all the ladies loved him; unfortunately he didn't love any one of them in return; and that was the cause of his later troubles."

Laughing Tomo added, "Yeah, the fathers in the village all hated him."

Gran gave a small smile. "Eventually even he found someone he couldn't ignore, and so he finally did fall in love; with the one girl he couldn't have."

"The daughter of Lord Stebron," Tomo commented.

"True, and a beautiful lass she was, and more than a little taken by Mute in return, though she knew her place in society and only used him as a plaything. But that boy; he couldn't let her go."

"Her father had him beaten."

"Yes, more than once. At first Stebron thought it was cute, and didn't really try to have the boy injured, but later..."

"The beatings got worse."

"And they got worse, until Mute snapped."

"He beat Lord Stebron and both his sons, then went on to whip Sir Miles and two men from the stable before they stopped him."

"Strong, he was, and is, and a ferocious fighter when his blood is up."

"Terrible temper," Tomo agreed.

"So that's why he's wanted?" Jamus asked.

"That's the beginning," Gran replied. "But only the beginning. He rotted in the Lord's dungeon for a year before he escaped; he lost so much weight that he was able to smear himself with bacon fat and squeeze between the bars. He hid in the forest naked for two months before he saw his chance."

"The Lord and his family were going on a hunt, and Mute followed them to the same area where Cobble is now... or was," Tomo looked pained. A lot of people he knew likely died when the invasion passed through there.

"Somehow he caught the Lord and his daughter alone and he challenged the man to a fight," she continued, only to be interrupted again by Tomo.

"Beat that man like an old drum."

"And then the girl told him that she would never run away with him, and that's when the Quargs took them."

Gran got silent then, tears brimming in her eyes until they began trickling down here cheeks. "And they hurt Mute bad, real bad. Ripped out his throat after torturing him for two days, and then left him to die."

"But he didn't die," stated Tomo.

"That he didn't," Gran growled, pulling herself up and glaring Jamus in the eye as if daring him to dispute her. "He lived, and rescued that girl and brought her home."

"But not until after the Quargs had had their way with her for months, more than a year, actually."

"True, and her father blamed Mute for it. He's been wanted ever since, and took other names to keep Lord Stebron from finding him."

"There are wanted men and then there are really wanted men," Tomo commented ruefully. "And the daughter would have nothing to do with him even after he rescued her."

"And just like many men have, once he was rejected he didn't even bother to try and clear his name. He disappeared into the wilderness and took his rage out on the Quargs. Occasionally he would get angry and return to the Stebron estates and take something special that belonged to the Lord. Sometimes he would deface it, like painting over a painting. Later he began stealing things to sell. Always he left something to tell Stebron who it was that had visited him."

"But he didn't keep the money; he gave it all to the poor."

"And if things had continued as they were it would have been bad enough, but then Stebron's oldest son caught Mute in one of his midnight raids. They fought, and the Lord's son died."

Jamus was nodding now. "I've heard this story; I knew Lord Stebron well, before he died. He hated Mute above all else, but his version of the story was quite different."

Gran pulled out her switch. "And my version of the story is the truth," she growled, brandishing the weapon.

"Of course, Gran, I never doubted you I was just noting the differences," Jamus protested, inching back until he hoped he was out of reach. "But once he was wanted for that many crimes, what difference did a name change make?"

"It mattered because Lord Stebron had more money than a man ought to," Gran groused. "Have you ever heard of a Diviner?"

Surprised Jamus nodded. "Yes I have, and that tells me a great deal. I know that they claim to be able to find anyone, anywhere, if you can provide them with a name. I don't really understand how it works."

"It works, I know that personally," commented Tomo ruefully.

"Magic is strange, but it has its uses," Gran said, acting as if she were agreeing with them though neither man knew exactly what she meant. "The Diviners have the ability to cast a massive, powerful spell that allows one of their order to know whenever a particular name is spoken. If you say that name, eventually you will be visited by a member of the Diviners."

"Gran had fun with it at first; she had me and two or three others travel all over the place saying the name," Tomo grinned. "Until the Diviners caught up to me; best beating I've had since before my older brother got married."

"It got so that anyone with that name changed it, and I haven't heard of a single child being named it since," Gran added. "Later Stebron learned of the new name Mute was using, and had the Diviners add that name to their search. That's why we don't use it, even after all these years. The spell is still in effect."

Sitting back against a tree Jamus took a long drink of icy water from a flask. The story they were telling was well known, as was the name of the central character. He hadn't believed it was true, nor had he imagined that he would ever meet that person.

"Well, I guess I know his name now," Jamus said. "Everyone knows that story."

"And we're trusting you not to say it or ever repeat what we've told you," Tomo added. "You and I have already discussed what will happen."

"Yes, you'll kill me," Jamus smiled. "Or one of Gran's other followers will."

"Good boys all of them," Gran added. "But I don't send people to kill others; I take care of that sort of thing myself."

Tomo looked uncomfortable at the woman's words but said, "That threat was all my own, my lord; I will kill you."

Realizing that the title was meant to increase the threat, Jamus sat forward and looked each of the others in the eye by turns. "You can count on me; I can keep a secret."

Harrumphing loudly Gran stated, "If there was any chance that you couldn't you wouldn't have been told."

Thanking her Jamus asked, "So Mute grew up in the same village as you, Tomo?"

Tomo tried to reply but Gran cut him off. "I said I was going to tell you about him and I will. Mute wasn't just one of my boy's, and there are a number of girls who have worked for me over the years, he was special."

"You said that; he was good at everything he put his hand too."

Scoffing at the viscount's words Gran replied, "I said that; it doesn't need to be repeated. But Mute is special in one other way." She began to cry.

Casting his eyes down like Tomo's already were Jamus waited out the moments of silence, allowing Gran to regain her composure. Finally she stifled her sobs and used the tip of her switch to gently prod Jamus beneath the chin. Once he lifted his head and met her gaze, she finished her thought.

"He's my son."

# Chapter Twenty-Seven

Two weeks later Gran led the way down the center of the main street of a small town named Gabelzedor, which meant 'green waving billows of unripe wheat' in old elvish, looking at the various signs hanging over the doors of the shops. Behind her came the rest of her small band; Tomo dragging the horse, Jamus pushing the horse, and a number of small children who had gathered thinking they were the lead elements of a traveling circus. Mute remained in the forest just in case; his wanted posters were posted here in Skallist as well.

Though they had marched steadily south the weather had gotten colder and the snow that eventually fell seemed to have decided to stay. The drifts were not large but the trails were covered to ankle depth and so traveling had gotten that much more difficult. Someone had to break trail for the horse; shuffling their feet through the snow to clear a path. If anything the poor animal's health had gotten worse and they were surprised it had made it this far.

An elvish town was strange to those unused to them. The buildings were narrow and uniform in height though of every color imaginable. A single door below and a single shuttered window above and a peaked roof sat touching one another, 'cheek by jowl' as Gran said, and could very well have been one long building on either side of the street. At least half of the buildings had no upper floor despite the window, as Tomo could see daylight shining through the shutters.

"What do the signs say, Gran?" asked Tomo, whose minimal reading skills did not extend to elvish.

Ignoring him Gran continued to puzzle out the signs, her lips moving as she translated using her minimal knowledge of the language. Though Gabelzedor was located well inside the borders of Skallist, an elven kingdom, most of the local population was human. In the spirit of keeping their superiors happy, the people of the town used elvish in all official capacities, such as the signs they used to identify their shops, but didn't always bother to spell the unfamiliar words correctly. When words in a foreign language were misspelled it made the translation more difficult, particular when it was elvish which had more than two hundred basic letters and nearly a thousand variants. Elvish also had more commonly used words than any other known language by a factor of ten, and each were highly descriptive. A single drop of paint from a careless brush could change a six letter elvish word meaning 'a shop of extensive products including blankets and things made of wool' to 'leather straps plied to beat the customers until they bleat like sheep.' Foreigners tended to be cautious about entering elvish shops.

"Ah, here's one," Gran stated at last. Pointing to a sign she read; "Dablefrkeysenthial." Turning to the others she translated, "A place of warmth and good ale where food can be found in exchange for coin and the beds customers sleep in are routinely checked for bugs."

Whistling, Tomo exclaimed, "Them elves sure get their money's worth out of a word, don't they?"

Jamus squinted up at the sign; being married to an elf had taught him a lot about the elvish language. "I bet the locals call it 'the Dabble'," he said.

Tying their horse to a post the three entered the building, which looked amazingly similar to every other building on the street and was hardly wide enough for three people to stand it in shoulder to shoulder. How it could be an inn with beds seemed to be beyond belief to Tomo, but he knew better than to question Gran with the mood she was in.

Within the building they found a small table and chair the only furniture of a tiny room. Another door was visible across from the one they had entered and on the table was a book, quill pen, and a bottle of ink. Tomo experimentally reached out to touch each wall, something he could do with his fingertips when standing still, as Jamus squeezed past Gran. Taking the quill in hand he signed the book with a flourish and then tapped the wind chime hanging from the ceiling. In seconds a small elven woman emerged from the other door, giving Tomo enough of a glimpse so that he knew it led back outside, and bowed to them. Glancing at the book she greeted Jamus by his title and asked them to step back outside.

"What happened?" demanded Tomo once they were back on the street. "Why did she kick us out?"

Gran looked as confused as Tomo but she said nothing, merely glaring at the viscount as she waited for his explanation.

"She didn't kick us out; this is just the room where you sign the ledger. Someone will be here momentarily to guide us to our rooms and then show us where to eat."

"It's not in the same building?" Tomo demanded.

Laughing the nobleman explained. "Elves aren't much into large structures. Everything they build is designed for a specific purpose and is never any larger than it has to be. Some of these buildings will be dining rooms, and there will be one table in it. Others will have a bed and a ladder that will lead up to another bed. If a lot of people need to gather, they do that outside."

"Ridiculous," Gran sniffed. "I've always said that elves are a strange lot and it looks like they're worse than that, like as not."

"They are different, I agree," said Jamus ruefully. "Of course, not everyone in this town is an elf, so there will be some 'normal' buildings about, but the elves frown upon them, and likely keep the main street as elvish as possible."

Soon a small human girl came out of a nearby doorway and motioned for them to follow her. She skipped happily along before them a few dozen buildings before stopping at a blue one with a bright yellow door. Obligingly the three stripped the horse and carried their things inside where, just as Jamus had said, there was a bed, table, chair and a ladder leading up to an exact duplicate room above. A back door led out back outside and there Tomo found a long trench that seemed to run parallel to every building on that side of the street. Stepping closer he discovered it to be a common privy.

"Gentlemen upstairs, I assume," Jamus said, bowing deeply to Gran, who responded by kicking him lightly in the backside as he climbed the ladder with his meager things.

With their possessions dropped into convenient corners the three reemerged to find the girl waiting for them, and then followed her again down a side street, a small bridge crossed the public privy-ditch that extended across the road itself, and eventually to a small barn. There they turned their horse over to an elvish hostler who misunderstood Jamus' command to 'take care of the horse' and had to be restrained from slitting the animal's throat.

"He said it was the kindest way to take care of it," the little girl translated. Once the misunderstanding was straightened out the girl danced along before them as they were led to another building and there fed a meal of oat cakes, honey, and little bits of meat deep-fried inside shredded okra. Gran wouldn't touch the meat until Tomo had identified it as squirrel. When their meal was complete the little girl was still waiting for them.

"Where to, my lord?" she asked cheerfully, giving her best curtsy.

"A tavern or a drinking room," Tomo said quickly. "I haven't been able to slake my thirst in a long time."

To the surprise of both men, Gran not only didn't complain but even offered to go along.

"Someone has to keep you children from trouble," she stated.

Again the three were led through the town by the skipping girl. The building they came to was blue with a yellow door again, making Tomo think that they had retraced their steps to their rooms, but they passed completely through that empty building and into the back, crossed a narrow bridge built across the privy trench, and entered an area filled with tables and chairs beneath the wide-spread limbs of a dozen or more trees. Tall stones at each corner of the area glowed a pinkish color and the snow within their boundaries was melted. The area was, indeed, quite comfortable and even Gran eventually loosened her cloak. They were alone save for the proprietor behind his bar and a handful of servers who sat together talking quietly and so chose a table close to one of the warming stones. Their guide sat quietly with them until Jamus assured her that they could find their rooms on their own. Her tip clutched in one hand she smiled, curtsied and then skipped away.

Jamus ordered drinks for them all, apparently his elvish was sufficient for that, and soon they were sipping their hot ciders as various locals began to arrive.

It felt wonderful to sit there, sipping a hot beverage as the warmth from the magical stones seeped into their bones. Gran even became somewhat mellow, and relaxed enough to stretch out her feet beneath the table. The proprietor, a human named Samlus, doted on them and kept a constant flow of servers passing their table.

"We're probably the only customers in the place with actual coin," Jamus explained. "Small town like this they mostly just barter." It was the last clear words he spoke the rest of the evening, as he was drinking more than his companions were combined and he was not contenting himself with cider. Already his words were beginning to slur and he had regained that vapid look in his eyes that Gran well remembered from their meeting in the Jackdog.

Gran sniffed. "You don't have to tell us about that, boy. We've lived in places smaller than this most of our lives."

Soon the sun began to go down and the gradually arriving clientele started getting more boisterous. One fight broke out, easily handled by the experienced Samlus as he tossed both men into the privy, and the quiet the travelers had enjoyed when first they arrived was long gone. At some point a young elf arrived with lyre in hand and, climbing a tree to perch upon a platform built there, began to serenade the audience with her sweet voice. Jamus immediately began singing with her; always knowing the right words to each song but seemingly getting the various verses out of order, until the woman gave up and left. Agreeing to have but one more drink before retiring for the night Tomo slipped out to use the privy as Jamus was ordering.

Finding himself in plain sight of everyone in the open-air tavern, Tomo walked a short distance into the deepening darkness and did his best to hide behind the bole of one of the trees. As he passed around it he found a number of placards and bits of weathered paper nailed to it, some of the older ones had worked a corner loose and were flapping in the chilling breeze. From the corner of his eye Tomo saw one that looked familiar and stopped to admire the caricature of Mute, laughing quietly at the horrid, evil face with a mouth full of fangs and eyes too large for his head. A few steps further around the tree his laughter stopped when he saw an equally unflattering picture of Gran.

There were several more of them tacked to the tree; all declaring that the woman named Gran was a wanted fugitive and had a price on her head. As quietly as possible Tomo gathered them all and shoved them into his shirt. Once he returned to the table he fully intended to urge his companions into leaving before anyone recognized her, but while cutting through a 'wall' of the tavern he passed near several tables of strangers on and his unexpected return from that direction allowed him to overhear a couple of words from each table, though the conversation died as soon as he was seen.

"... with a reward that big I could..."

"...dump the old woman and get me..."

"...sitting right there as bold as brass and a murderer..."

"...look out, he's with her!"

"We need to leave, right now," he muttered to Gran as he reached the table.

"I'm not ready to leave," she snarled. "I'm just now beginning to feel my toes again."

Seeing the look in Tomo's face, Jamus got immediately to his feet. "I'll go settle up with the owner," he said without preamble. His words were heavily slurred and his footing none too sure as he weaved off to find Samlus.

"I said I'm not leaving," Gran growled, squinting at the back of the retreating nobleman but speaking to Tomo. "What's your hurry? I didn't figure on being able to pry you away from this place until morning."

Trying to be as surreptitious as possible, Tomo slid one of the wanted posters from his shirt and showed it to her; the open-mouthed snarl of the caricature visible only for a moment before he stuffed it back in.

Gran sniffed. "I don't know what you're worried about; that picture doesn't look anything like me," she argued, but got to her feet anyway.

"We've used your name all over town, Gran. You know we didn't figure the posters would have come this far south."

They stood and moved towards the bridge as Jamus cut across the floor to join them. Tomo eased the knife in his belt as he watched from the corner of his eyes three tables of patrons standing to leave when they did.

"Uh-oh," Tomo whispered. "We're about to be followed."

Just as they crossed the bridge the viscount caught up to them, weaving slightly from the harder alcohol he'd been drinking liberally since their arrival. He had another bottle in one hand and was beginning to sing something in elvish that had half the people in the tavern looking ill and the other half insulted. Either way the nobleman was unaware and had fallen into his old speech patterns.

"Ick! Peasants all about me," he slurred, pausing to look goggle-eyed at a portly human with a hair-lip. "Come along old woman, you'll need to turn down my blankets for me; I don't believe I can manage it in my state," he giggled, weaving into Tomo.

"You'll turn down your own blankets, you sot," Gran whispered, trying her best to avoid any further attention than they were already drawing.

"How did he get drunk so fast?" Tomo whispered to Gran as he worked his head beneath one of the Jamus' arms and levered the man to a more upright position.

"He's a slave to bottled spirits, like as not, and being without for so long made his resistance low," Gran sniffed, looking unsure whether she should produce her switch or not. "Let's get him back to the room."

"We can't go back there, Gran, that's the first place they'll look," Tomo whispered as he followed the woman back through the house and onto the street. "They'll trap us there for sure."

Now the switch appeared and Gran gave Tomo a solid whack across one thigh. "Don't you think I know that? But we have to go back; all our supplies and whatever coin this sot hasn't drunk up are there. If we leave town without our supplies we won't live to reach the next one."

"I don't know about that Gran, I bet Mute could keep us alive even if I couldn't. There's food to be had in the woods, even in wintertime."

That made Gran think for a moment, she was even quiet, but ultimately dismissed the idea. "No, we'd never make it out of town with that rabble following us," she stated, pointing vaguely over one shoulder. She could see that Tomo was already getting tired and couldn't carry the viscount much further. "They're probably trying to circle around and get ahead of us too; best we get somewhere they can't surprise us. At least in our room they won't dare burn us out; they'd destroy half the town."

Unsure whether to argue, Tomo felt much safer in the wilds than he did in a town, years of obeying Gran won out and he dropped the subject. Concentrating on keeping the almost limp Jamus on his feet took up most of his attention anyway, and the woodsman was exhausted when Gran finally opened a door. Expecting to see that she had chosen the wrong room, Tomo was relived to see their gear piled in a corner.

"Get him upstairs," Gran ordered as she dug into one pack and Tomo locked the doors. "I don't need him underfoot if it comes to a fight."

"Yes Gran," Tomo panted, shoving the other man into the ladder hard enough to either wake him or knock him out, thankfully it accomplished the former and Jamus grabbed onto a rung for support. Mumbling in protest the nobleman seemed to climb out of reflex, Tomo following closely behind to prevent him from falling. Once the man was successfully deposited face-first onto the bed, Tomo made sure that the shutters were bolted and then dug into his own gear.

Regretfully he left his bow there, this would likely be close up work, and chose instead a hatchet he used to trim firewood for tender. That and his belt knife would have to do. When he came back down the ladder he saw Gran gripping the frying pan Tomo had brought with him when he fled Cobble. It was the same one she had dipped in the molten silver in order to fight the Were that had killed her son Borel and bitten Albrim. Despite the obvious humor in seeing an elderly woman armed only with a frying pan, Tomo couldn't help but be glad it wasn't he who had to face her.

"You bolt the shutters?" she demanded.

"Yes Gran, and they're right over the bed so if anyone does get in that way, they'll have to step on Jamus to get down here."

"At least the sot is good for something," Gran grumped.

"Well, he is paying for everything," Tomo offered. Despite his threats to kill the man if he ever revealed the truth about Mute, he really liked the noble.

Gran wasn't to be discouraged. "Money he has and that's all, like as not. No common sense, no courage, he's got to contribute what he can."

"He seems alright to me, Gran, but all the same I wish Mute was here."

"Might as well wish for the dead to live again, Tomo. He's too far away to know what's going on."

Whatever else she might have been intending to say was lost when a solid thump sounded from the back door. Cautiously Tomo unbolted it and peered through the smallest crack he could manage. An arrow was driven into the solid wood, and a scrap of parchment was impaled upon the shaft. Peering around as best he could, Tomo saw no one close to the door, so he reached out and wiggled the missile free. Once the door was securely bolted again, he handed the note over to Gran. On one side was a brief note scrawled in elvish; on the reverse was the wanted poster for Gran.

"Surrender to us and we'll let you live," she read. "Fools, they misspelled more than half the words."

Another thump sounded, this time on the front door. Following the same procedure as before, Tomo found another note there and retrieved it.

"Humph, this one is even worse," Gran sniffed. "Surrender to us and not to them other guys or we'll kill you really dead."

"So I guess we're surrounded," Tomo offered, aware even as he said it that he would shortly be subject to a tongue-lashing by Gran for stating the obvious. To his surprise she said nothing.

Stalking in a circle, Gran tapped a finger to her chin; a classic sign that she was pondering her alternatives. Finally she shared her thoughts; "We're surrounded, but by two different groups that are opposed to one another. That might give us an advantage," she began. Then the head of an axe broke through the front door.

# Chapter Twenty-Eight

Having no time to think it all the way through, Tomo leaped into action. Drawing the hatchet from his belt he turned to the nearest wall and brought the weapon down hard. To his surprise, he broke through easily and his hand up to the elbow burst through the flimsy panel. Looking back at Gran in happy surprise, he turned and forced his way through the wall just as the front door gave way from the blows of the axe. Tomo considered trying the next wall but knew that their pursuers would be upon them before they could escape. Reaching back through the hole he grabbed Gran by the arm, dragging her through after him and sending her sprawling onto the floor. Standing across the opening Tomo yelled for Gran to bar the doors of the new room, it was a mirror of the one they had just left, and stood watching for his first attacker to appear. Long moments passed with no one showing before Tomo cautiously stepped back into the original room.

The front door was in splinters; he could see the buildings across the street plainly, but no one had tried yet to reach through to lift away the bar. The snow on the ground was reflecting the light of one of the moons and details directly in front of the hole made by the ax were as clear as daylight. The ax used on the door lay in the snow. Nearby were drops of something dark... blood!

Throwing caution to the wind Tomo rushed to the broken portal and peered out; there were more than a few spots of blood on the ground; there was also a hand. Stepping to his left he followed it upwards finding the arm, then the back of a man's head. Just below his neck the head of an arrow was visible pushing out through his back.

"It's Mute," Tomo whooped, looking back at Gran. "He must be outside, watching us."

Gran joined him, looking out the hole at the dead ax man. "How can you be sure?" she demanded.

"I recognize the arrow; it's one of those we bought in Vicksville."

Saying nothing more the two took turns watching out the broken door but no further attackers were seen. Neither did Mute make an appearance. When the sun finally grew close to the horizon Gran sent Tomo up the ladder to rouse their drunken companion. The woodsman found the viscount in the same position he had left the man hours before; facedown on the bed and snoring loudly. Waking Jamus was not easy, but Tomo managed it by throwing open the shutters and allowing the frigid night air to do the job for him. Cursing and whining the noble crawled to his feet, holding his head with one hand as he used the other to keep himself from falling. Gran was her usual tolerant self concerning the hangover, and had the man dressed, packed, and waiting outside within minutes of his waking. By the time the sun finally made its first appearance, the travelers had recovered their horse and put the town behind them; the streets conspicuously empty even considering the early hour, and they were back in the hopeful safety of the forest.

"They'll be following us for sure, Gran," Tomo said. "I saw at least four blood trails, counting the dead man by the door. Someone won't like that."

"I don't care what they like; it was self defense and nothing more. We left coin enough to pay for the wall and the door; burying the dead is their problem."

Knowing when to drop a subject, Tomo grew quiet. It wasn't exactly clear to him that self defense would matter when the men killed were trying to capture someone already wanted for murder. Shortly after that he left Gran with the still groaning Jamus leading the horse and fell back to watch their back trail.

It was snowing again, so all they needed was time to conceal their trail. He had changed directions every time he had found a new path through the forest; once even backtracking towards the town for a short while to further confuse any pursuit. So far he had seen no one but that bothered him even more; people had died in Gabelzedor, and that wasn't usually tolerated by officials whose livelihood was based on keeping the locals both happy and alive.

Unsure why there was no pursuit Tomo had to grudgingly accept the fact that they had escaped and turned back towards the southeast, the direction Gran insisted upon, and urged his companions to make as much speed as they could manage. Around noon Mute caught up to them, jogging through the forest to intercept them on their current path. The fact that he didn't bother to conceal his own trail was a great relief to Tomo.

After exchanging greetings they continued moving at Mute's insistence, the woodsman telling Gran that there were search parties looking for them.

"You led them off another direction?" Tomo asked. Mute nodded, warning the others that the searchers were numerous but, for now, were looking in the wrong direction.

"You're a wonder, Mute," Jamus exclaimed. "Thanks for leading them away."

Mute waved the compliment away, reaching out with one hand to hug Gran to him as way of explanation.

"And thanks for helping us last night," Tomo added. "You saved us for sure."

This time Mute look confused, and shrugged.

"He doesn't know what you're talking about," Gran translated.

"The men that attacked us?" Tomo asked.

Again the big man shrugged, his eyes showing both alarm and confusion as his hands worked furiously.

Gran answered him. "Now stop that; we had a little trouble and that's all. But we did have help; are you saying it wasn't you?"

Shaking his head, Mute demanded the story. After it had been related to him by Tomo he dropped his head, obviously thinking hard as he walked. Then he asked a number of questions through Gran that revealed every detail of the previous night he could wring from them. Suspiciously he pointed at Jamus.

"Ow, don't point so loud," the noble groaned, whimpering as he held his head.

"It wasn't him, Mute," Tomo explained. "He was passed out upstairs; he couldn't have gotten past us, then across the street to kill three men, fire an arrow back towards us, and then get back upstairs without us seeing him."

Snorting loudly Gran agreed. "The man was worse that usual; look somewhere else for a hero, my boy."

Shaking his head Tomo changed the subject. "And this may not be the first time this has happened." Turning to Mute he asked, "Back in Vicksville, when those men tried to come at us in the hospital that last night, did you follow them?"

Mute shook his head again.

"What are you getting at, Tomo?" Gran demanded. "They were thieves, like as not, and left when they didn't find anything."

"No Gran, they weren't thieves. After they left they came back around to the wall outside of Mute's bed, and they talked about 'the old woman sleeps right here' and that they were 'coming back to finish the job'. They were there to kill you, Gran."

Mute nodded his agreement, pointing at Gran and drawing a finger across his throat.

"The next morning two men were found dead in an alley."

Gran sniffed, but she didn't look as confident as she tried to sound. "Coincidence, nothing more. Two poor souls killed for their cloaks or a copper in their pocket, like as not."

Turning the old woman left the men behind as she snatched the reins from Jamus and stalked on, leaving them to share a look of concern.

"I don't like it, Mute. Someone is helping us, and that's fine, but somehow they're trailing along without you or me either one noticing them," Tomo whispered. "That stinks of sorcery or worse. Who knows what that sort have in mind? Help us today; sacrifice us to some demon or another tomorrow."

Mute looked doubtful about some of Tomo's tirade but nodded his head in acceptance anyway. It bothered him that someone could follow them without his knowledge, even if they did have magic on their side.

Taking turn about Mute and Tomo were as careful as they could be over the following days. They took turns concealing their trail and used every trick they knew to throw off any pursuit, even circling back occasionally to watch for anyone following. Mute, at least once each day, would use a low-hanging limb to scramble up into a forest giant and lay hidden on a high branch for hours to watch, just in case. They saw nothing; not even other travelers or refugees and circled wide around to avoid the various small villages and homes they encountered. Whatever the troubles in the north it seemed to have nothing to do with this part of Skallist, and the land was peaceful. Ten days out of Gabelzedor Mute and Tomo were satisfied that if anyone had followed them, they were now far behind and surely had lost their trail.

On the eleventh day they began to approach the city of Afstakanalzenorg, the second largest city in all of Skallist and the first major population center south of Aldrigal. It was also right on the road Gran and Jamus had been traveling when the Were had attacked their carriage. Unable to completely avoid the thousands that lived in the area, they still were careful to avoid as much attention as possible and took three full days to circle the city to the south. Disdaining inns, they continued to rough it, sending Jamus into town to replenish their supplies as necessary and to pick up some extra weapons. Using his name he replenished his funds as well, and bought a decent packhorse to replace the one that had finally died one night along the trail. When they were on the southwestern edge of the city they left the forest and began traveling along a decent road for the first time in weeks and covered more distance in the next two days than they had in some weeks. Even their new horse showed more spirit, prompting comments from Tomo that the 'old nag was making good time', followed by Jamus quipping 'better be quiet, Tomo, Gran is only a little bit deaf.'

Wearing a thicker cloak purchased for her by Jamus, one with a deep hood, Gran felt comfortable walking along the road so long as she kept her face covered and, less often, her voice down. Mute continued to follow them at a distance, rarely using the highway itself but still keeping from sight as only he could. About noon of the third day out of the city Gran ordered a change of direction, and the group followed a narrow trail to the northwest that grew narrower as they followed it back towards the mountains. They camped that night inside an abandoned temple as even more snow fell.

"I don't mean to be intruding, Gran," Jamus asked after drawing the short straw. "but where exactly are we going?"

Giving her characteristic sniff she replied, "As if you've ever cared where you were or where you were going. You're lazy and shiftless, boy, and have wasted your whole life wandering about." She growled, and then totally against her usual character went on to answer him. "If you must know we're going to the convent of St. Lacitor."

"Never heard of that one, Gran. Who was St. Lacitor?"

"Are you going to become a priestess, Gran?" snickered Tomo.

After switching a laughing apology from Tomo Gran replied to the viscount. "St. Lacitor was a drunkard and worse, but he had the good fortune to die in the right place at the right time, because a few so-called miracles happened close enough to his grave that he got all the credit. All I care about is that the current Abbess is literate and her order tends to keep written records of current events."

Confused Jamus asked, "Why is a convent named after a man?"

"Because no priests would build a monastery to St. Lacitor. He was hated, even loathed, by every man who ever met him. When he drank, which was constantly, he liked to fight and apparently did that very well. Only the priestesses of his order revere him."

Despite considerable efforts at trying to learn more from Gran as to why they were here, the men had no success. Early the next morning she left them behind and traveled the final mile on foot to the convent. Warned not to expect her immediate return, the three men spent a quiet and cold night together, though a pair of priestesses from the convent did bring them a hot meal. In mid-afternoon of the next day Gran arrived, kicking a slumbering Jamus from his blankets and ordering them to break camp.

"I've got 'em," she cackled, over and over. "Douse that fire, Tomo; I've got 'em! Mute, find us a trail heading due west, I've got 'em! Jamus put your pants on, boy! We've got to get a move on!"

# Chapter Twenty-Nine

General Handrick watched the fires burning along the waterfront, pleased to see the Aldrigalian vessels they had caught at the docks being consumed by the conflagration. The tall flames against the backdrop of the falling snow were beautiful in a way. No one knew better than he just how tenuous the Firthian hold was on Aldrigal, and the more damage they could do now before the snow made travel impossible would make all the difference in whether or not they could hold it in the spring; commanding the waterways would be important. So far things were going as well as he could have hoped; but much more needed to be accomplished.

"Nazrigal is yours, my lord," shouted a Firthian messenger. His excitement was palpable and all those clustered around the Were echoed his enthusiasm save for the Grand Liaison; the obese fellow just giggled in his saddle.

"The looting has already begun," laughed Azchod, the Were watching as mercenaries emerged from a nearby home with their arms full of plunder.

Cursing the greed of the mercenaries Handrick looked around for any of the mercenary captains. He hadn't really expected to see any; with plunder available they would be out with their men.

"The fools," he snarled. "I told them no plunder until the city was secured; there are still pockets of resistance on the hill," the general growled.

"My men will take care of that, General," announced Colonel von Tirek, the commander of the Firthian Spears.

Handrick ignored the man. He did not want to publicly state that he would rather lose mercenaries than loyal Firthian troops, but that was how the assault of the city had been planned. Mercenary companies were easily replaced, particularly when the plunder was as rich as what had been found in Aldrigal, but the Firthian troops could not be thrown away without cause.

"Where next, General?" asked Azchod. "We've the two largest cities in the southern half of Aldrigal under control, including the capitol and the river port. Is this where we'll winter or do you plan to move on?"

With the smell of freshly spilled blood so strong on the air, Handrick was having trouble remaining in his human form. Azchod had not even bothered to hold back, and had been in the upright wolf form throughout the battle; making the horses of everyone in the command group nervous. Slowly the horses captured in Aldrigal were getting used to the Weres in human form, but their scent was not as strong as when fully wolf.

"You know the plan, Azchod, the same as I do. We move on to Taramont in the morning, even if we have to burn the whole city before we go." Handrick paused before making a decision. "Azchod, take our brethren up the hill, help the soldiers there clean out the resistance."

Smiling the Were turned to where the other Weres were clustered and waved for them to follow him. They left their horses behind and were in full wolf form before they were out of Handrick's sight.

"Speaking of resistance, General, what is the latest news out of Aldrigal City?" asked von Tirek. "Has General Intona had any more success in rooting them out?"

Waving for an aide to answer, Handrick returned to admiring the flames. Clearing his throat the young messenger spoke.

"General Intona has sent word that he has had continued success at putting down the rebels, but that the threat remains. He has asked for more troops, claiming that he has not enough men to control the population."

Boastfully von Tirek said, "General Intona is a fine soldier; if he believes that he needs more troops, they should be given to him."

"There are no more troops to send, at least not until spring," stated Handrick. "We need every man here if we are to bottle up the fortress at Taramont, and no time to waste in doing so."

"General, do you think we can get the men moving by morning?" asked von Tirek, miffed that it was not he dispatched to finish the last defenders as well as having his suggestion rebuffed so callously. "We'll not be able to roust out the mercenaries in the morning; likely they'll be out pillaging all night."

Nodding Handrick had to agree. "You are probably right, Colonel, but we will try. Our main focus is to get to Taramont as soon as possible; and keep forces from the northern cities from crossing there. We don't need all our forces to prevent that, so we'll wait a day and leave with what we have. You, Colonel, will remain here as governor of the city, and see to its welfare on behalf of Firth."

Stunned the young Colonel could only stare at the Were, and then nod dumbly as he saluted. Handrick couldn't help but smile; he was slowly ridding himself of the officers he did not trust or like by assigning them to just this sort of position. Technically it was a promotion, but to a young officer it had to be terribly disappointing.

"I thank you, general, for your trust. Might I inquire as to how many men I'll be given to accomplish this task?"

"Far less than you'll want," laughed Handrick. "But enough to do the deed. I'll need every able bodied man I can get for Taramont."

"But general, surely we don't have enough troops to take the castle, and the winter is too far along for a siege. Wouldn't it be more prudent, as well as militarily sound, to winter here? Or in Aldrigal City and strengthen our hold there?"

Almost Handrick ignored the young Colonel's words. Almost he revealed the plans that would see them not only besieging the fortress of Taramont, but taking it within days of their arrival. Almost.

# Chapter Thirty

"From village, to wilderness, to cities and back to wilderness again," groused Jamus. "Where is she taking us now?"

Glancing at the noble Tomo replied. "You could have left us at any time. You didn't have to trail along."

"What? And deny you my company and my vast wilderness skills?" laughed Jamus. "Without my deep pockets you would all have starved long ago. Besides," he sobered, "my wife wanted to help Gran, and so I'm going to help her."

The last home was long behind them and the southern range of the Kenebruks were now hanging over them. On some maps, they were already among them, though they now traveled between two outthrust arms of the mountains and they had not actually had to ascend much. The snow was deep and getting deeper by the day; the worst winter thus far than even Gran could recall.

"Then why didn't you buy horses for all of us? And a score or two of bodyguards? Tomo demanded. "You've got the coin; we've certainly got the need."

Jamus rolled his eyes. "I offered, many times, but Gran always says 'no'. Says we don't the attention nor the extra mouths to feed. We could have been here days ago, a week or more, if I'd bought horses, but she threatened to switch me if I did."

Slogging a few more steps on the snowshoes he had made Tomo grumbled. "I wish you'd just bought the horses; switchings heal quicker than frostbit toes."

The narrow path they had been following, actually nothing more than an abnormally wide space between the leaf-bare trees, threatened to peter out to nothing several times but somehow they continued to move the direction Gran wanted; now north and west. Then, to everyone's surprise, a full-blown road of packed earth and stones appeared before them, swept clean of snow as if a strong southern breeze had blown for days. There on the dry roadbed, standing between the high snowdrifts to either side, Mute awaited them. He did not look happy and began working his fingers as soon as he caught sight of Gran.

"Yes, yes, I know it's not natural for the road to be clear; it's magic, boy, and that's why we're here," she explained, leading the pack horse around her son and plodding on up the road is if it were normal to find it clear when the forest all about was choked with snow.

Uneasy with the situation the others followed along quietly, even Mute remaining with them instead of disappearing into the forest to scout for enemies. Each of the men kept a weapon handy, with both of the woodsmen stringing their bows and keeping an arrow ready to the string. Gran stumped on ahead as if on her way to hoe her garden. Soon a tower appeared above the bare trees and soon after, another. A twin to the first save that one side had collapsed. Finally the trees fell away to either side and a large stone and wood-timbered building appeared, the towers a part of the structure that looked to have been, at one time, at least three stories high. Much of the building, including most of the upper floor, had fallen and trees of some size were growing around, and even through in one place, the structure. It had obviously been abandoned for decades.

"What is this place, Gran?" Tomo wondered.

"It was once a place of study, and learning," she replied, tying off the horse to a body of a small dead pine.

"I don't like the feel of the place," added Jamus.

Gran spat. "It wasn't knowledge you'd like to be involved in, Jamus. Experiments performed here were often performed on unwilling human subjects, and they rarely survived." She sniffed, "And rarely wanted to as well, like as not."

Dead vines covered part of the wall but the snow-cleared road turned into a snow-cleared walkway that led up to a forbidding front door made of a single piece of iron. A brass frame on the door held a sign and just above it was a tiny brass bell centered in a symbol of some type. The symbol was circular and contained what looked like the profile of a tree. Gran stalked directly to the door and made a show of reading the sign.

"Touch nor enter not, for this door is trapped and warded against all intrusions," she read. "Looks like the same thing written in at least three languages I recognize, and a few I don't."

"I recognize four or five myself," offered Jamus. "And I can feel the magic in that door; likely we're supposed to."

"The hairs on my arms are standing up," offered Tomo.

"It's heavily warded, that's certain," Gran stated. "But we need to get past this door, and get past it we will, like as not. Just give me a moment to think."

Mute stepped up and tapped Gran on the shoulder. Finally he gained her attention and pointed to a large hole in the wall at the far corner.

Switching Mute out of her way Gran exclaimed, "I know that, boy. I haven't lived the last ten years in a tree."

Smiling the three men followed her to the hole, created when a tree fell against the wall years ago, and entered the building. The first room was large and filled with snow-covered debris and no part of the floor was clear. Scrambling over the pile they saw the upper portion of a fireplace and two other doorways half-choked with debris. The ceiling was missing here, and the upper floors were also open to the weather. The tree they had seen growing from within the building stood in one corner.

Motioning for the men to hold back, Gran looked through each of the doorways. Making her choice she waved them along and led the way deeper into the structure. The next room was in better shape with only a single hole in one wall. It had been a kitchen based on the large copper pot found tarnishing atop a stove. Squirrels and moks had made nests there over the years and a particularly large rat peered sleepily at them from its nest in one corner. Two other doorways in the kitchen led to pantries that had been cleared out before the building fell into disrepair.

"Clear that oven and build a fire," Gran ordered. "Fix us something hot to eat. We might be here a few days. We'll probably sleep here if we don't find anything better upstairs."

"At least we'll be out of the wind," stated Jamus.

Not replying Gran left them to get organized as she moved back into the first room and then out the other door. A hallway had a number of side chambers but she ignored them for the steep stairway she had seen at the far end. It was made of wood and looked to be in serious danger of collapse, but what she needed was more than likely up there so up she intended to go.

The crash of the falling timbers brought the others running. Dodging her switch and taking her curses the men quickly dug Gran out of the debris.

"I need to get up there," she snarled by way of explanation, and Mute nodded that he understood. Pointing at Tomo to get his attention, he sent the other woodsman back to the kitchen to retrieve something before nimbly shinnied up the wall using the rusty bolts that once held the stairs in place. Once there he lay on the upper floor and waited for Tomo to return with a piece of rope and a lit lantern. Tying one to the other he flipped the other end of the rope to Mute so that he could pull the lantern up. After taking a careful look around, a delay that Gran took in typical style by cursing and switching Jamus, the rope was returned and Gran was lifted easily up by the big man.

"Wait here," Gran huffed, pointing to the exact spot she wanted Mute to sit. "And you others get back to making camp! I want some hot tea ready by the time I come back down."

Mute refused, making slashing motions with his hands to indicate his concerns.

"There's nothing up here that I can't handle. Do you think that I'm scared of a mouse? Sit down there and wait for me; if I stumble across a dragon or a Quarg, I'll give you a yell."

Still chuckling at her fall now that they knew she wasn't hurt, Tomo and Jamus returned to the kitchen as Gran lifted up her lantern and followed along the upper hallway, Mute obediently sitting down on the floor. The rooms were mostly empty, as she expected, but some still had a few sticks of furniture. Two held the remnants of beds and in another a handful of dead bats hung from the rafters with the expected heap of guano below. The end of the hall ended in open air, looking down on the room they had originally entered, so Gran entered a room that opened again into another hallway that led to the back of the building. There she found a different brand of debris; broken beakers and jars that once held a variety of compounds. A stuffed lizard of tremendous size hung from rusted chains in the hallway itself and the place stank of sulfur and ammonia. There was guano here as well, but in only minute amounts, and the rats seemed to have taken control and built nests of straw and paper. Excited, Gran pushed on ahead.

Any windows that may have existed were well covered, for no light existed save that from the lantern. Shadows dipped and moved as her lantern fought a losing battle trying to drive away the thick shadows. Every movement by Gran, every swing by the lantern hanging from her fingers, caused the arms of chairs to become grasping fingers and their backs to become monsters intent on slipping up behind her for the kill. Despite her best intentions Gran felt a shiver up her spine at the sudden fear and cursed herself for her foolishness, but still she couldn't stop looking over her shoulder occasionally, just to be sure.

"Foolishness all," she complained. "I'm here for Albrim!" she said weakly, glaring into the darkness as if it would dare argue with her. "I'm here for Albrim!" she said again, this time a little louder. Repeating the words as her mantra Gran forced herself on, shining the light into each room in turn until she found what she was looking for; a rusty iron ladder leading further up.

Huffing like a bellows Gran slowly ascended the ladder. It opened up into a smallish room that had a desk and cabinets that were probably too large to bother moving, or stealing, when the original occupants had left. A quick search of the room turned up nothing of value save a single sheet of parchment showing a tree within a circle with smudges over the other details. She recognized it, certainly; it was the same symbol that had adorned the talisman she had found around the neck of the Were that came to Cobble. That was why she was here.

Sitting on the edge of the desk for a moment Gran took the time to regain her breath and rest her aching leg. Not for the first time she realized just how age could pull you down. Once her breathing had returned to normal she picked up her lantern and moved through the only door into a larger room, easily occupying perhaps half of the top floor. Long tables were set here and there, each covered in dust and thick with mildew from a leaky roof. The room was bone-chillingly cold, colder even than the air outside had been, and Gran suspected that the temperature was not entirely natural in origin. Picking through the tables she found nothing of interest, save for a larger version of the tree symbol burned into the wall, and moved on to the room's other door. This one was in better shape than most of those she had passed to this point, and she firmly gripped the wolf-headed handle to pull it open.

Another desk, another cabinet, a collapsed bookshelf and more cobwebs than Gran had ever seen in one place awaited her there. This time she was more careful about searching through the debris, and happily extracted several small, thin volumes from a pile beneath the bookshelf. Cackling in glee she stacked the six books together and bound them together with twine into an easily transportable bundle. Taking them under one arm she hurried back towards the sunlight.

"I'm going to save you yet, Albrim," she announced. No one heard her but the rats.

# Chapter Thirty-One

"We came all this way through the cold and snow for those?" laughed Tomo, not for the first time. Each time he saw the mildewed little books he found it funny.

"My wife lost her life for those," Jamus growled, glaring at the woodsman with uncharacteristic anger. "Do not make light of them."

Gran placated both men by taking up a morsel of the fresh bread they had baked in the restored oven and shoving it into each man's mouth.

"That'll be enough of that," she chided. "You leave the worth of these books up to me; I didn't come here for nothing."

Mute tapped the book in Gran's hand and asked why. Three days she had spent reading them without telling the men much of anything about them. Deciding that she had enough information to speak on, she relented.

"These books are the personal journals of Merceena, a wizard who lived a century ago," she began. "At one time she was an apprentice to Istipol, a Wizardess of Aldrigal. She was released from Istipol's service because of her evil nature." At this point Gran produced the drawing she had made of the talisman taken from the long-dead Were and held it next to the identical sign on the cover of one of the books. After explaining the drawing's origin she continued.

"After Merceena left Aldrigal she completed her apprenticeship with another wizard, an old man who lived alone in this area. When he died, Merceena took his small home as her own and began her own experiments. She had a fascination with Weres, and researched them almost exclusively. Occasionally she hired herself out to earn coin as a mercenary mage, and eventually made enough to build this place and take on her own apprentices."

"She must have liked her solitude," Jamus quipped, looking ashamed when Gran gave him 'the look'.

"Whether she did or not doesn't matter," Gran sniffed. "She had to have it because of what she was doing out here; nothing honest folk would put up with I assure you."

"How do you go about researching Weres? It wouldn't seem like they would be all that cooperative when it came to being experimented on," asked Tomo.

"They wouldn't at that, but there are ways, aren't there boy?" Gran replied, leaning over to pat Mute on the cheek. The big man turned red beneath his grubby beard at the praise but nodded. He'd handled Albrim easily enough during the boy's early transformations.

"But what is there to learn about Weres? Everyone knows how to kill them; was she looking for an easier way?" asked Tomo.

Shaking her head grimly Gran replied, "No, Tomo. She wasn't interested in killing them; she wanted to find a way to harness their power; to somehow be able to transfer their strength and healing ability to herself without taking on the negative aspects of the Curse as well. Plus finding a way to avoid the influence of the moons, which as far as I know isn't really understood."

Mute pantomimed a question and Gran nodded without translating.

"After a number of years Merceena died and her remaining apprentices stripped everything of value, at least the things they wanted and could carry, and moved away to other places. At least that is what Merceena herself expected to happen, and that's what she wrote in her journals more than once. They all hated her, and she despised them in turn, and not one of them wanted to spend any more time here in the wilderness than they had to. All of her research, all of her notes, were taken, naturally. The only written accounts left behind were these journals and they are of no value to anyone except me."

"So this is a dead end?" asked Tomo.

"Not at all," Gran cackled. "This symbol was all I had to begin with, and the library of Istipol led me here. Now I know that the symbol I search for was originally that of Merceena and must still be in use by one or more of her apprentices."

"But this apprentice isn't here anymore, so what good is the knowledge that they once were?" inquired Jamus.

"Because there are clues enough in these little books, despite the missing pages and others too mildewed to be read, that can tell anyone with half a brain where to look next. And I am that person," Gran exclaimed. Not realizing why the men all chuckled at her proclamation she continued. "Here in this book," she held up one volume that looked much like the others save for the pattern of mildew on the cover, "Merceena went on in great detail about her adventures as a mercenary. She would hire out to anyone with the coin, but she intentionally kept her price high to keep from being bothered with trivial matters. These periods of employment were important, of course, but she found them woefully boring and began hiring out her underlings in her place as quickly as she could get them trained. She claimed that most of her time on these expeditions was spent sitting, sleeping, and using her magic to enhance her employer's communications."

"Communications?" Tomo asked.

It was Jamus that replied. "Communications between groups is decidedly important in military matters; it can be the difference in victory or defeat, or so I've read."

"Quite right, Jamus. And Merceena soon developed a reputation to that effect; and several of her former employers recommended her for that use. Eventually, once her students had taken over the 'business' so to speak, she gave her little organization a name to reflect that specialty."

"The Signalers!" blurted Jamus.

"I've heard of them," stated Tomo excitedly. "A mercenary group of wizards; all women!"

"I haven't heard anything about them being involved with Weres; just that they're a pretty odd bunch of characters," the viscount added.

"We've all heard the stories," Gran cautioned, "but knowing the truth is not always the same thing. Just being a user of magic can make you seem odd to those who can't."

"I've seen one Signaller; she was in the pay of the Duke of Landsbridge," offered Jamus. "She didn't bathe or comb her hair; the rumors were that she didn't sleep either."

"Rumors again!" Gran scoffed. "The bathing part I believe, but not the other. What doesn't sleep doesn't live, like as not."

Mute snapped his fingers to gain Gran's attention before asking a question.

"From here we follow the trail of her former apprentices; the last ones listed here in her journals and so the ones most likely to have still been here when she died," Gran replied, patting the books in her lap. "In total there are four, but I believe we can narrow down the list somewhat. I'm pretty sure I recognize one of these names as having died in the Were War, and she wasn't a member of the Signalers."

Not for the first time the men exchanged a confused glance. The Were Wars were decades ago; just how old was Gran?

"But Gran what good is all of this?" Tomo asked; confusion plain on his face. "Even if we find the right apprentice, track her or her apprentices down, what good is that doing us?"

Placing a hand on Tomo's Gran met his eyes, looking like a teacher trying to relay a simple concept to her dullest pupil. "Merceena had an interest in Weres and the one that Cursed Albrim wore her symbol, or close enough not to matter. If any of her apprentices kept up her research, and it seems likely that at least one has, then they may know something that will help him."

"Gran, do you mean to say that you think someone may have discovered a cure to the Curse?"

"Perhaps," Gran sniffed, a tear trickling down one wrinkled cheek. "But if not, then perhaps they will at least have some knowledge that will help him take control of his changes; give him back some type of life."

Nodding his head gravely, Mute tapped his arm meaningfully at Gran.

"Yes Mute, there is that as well."

If the other men noticed the cryptic response, they didn't react.

"So we find this Were-loving apprentice and she just gives you the information you need?" asked Jamus. "I've pledged my resources to you Gran, but what if they don't want to sell?"

"Give it to me, barter it to me, or I'll just take it anyway that I can," Gran stated, the grim set of her jaw and the piercing strength of her best eye warning the noble not to take her words lightly. "No one that comes between me and my blood will last long enough to regret it!"

Tapping his arm again, Mute nodded sagely.

"Well what do you have in the way of information then, Gran?" Jamus asked.

Clearing her throat Gran opened one of the journals. "Four names; the last four apprentices that served Merceena. One is dead, and I'm relatively certain that she is not the one we need because I met her. She was strong in magic but I recall nothing of a symbol that looks like Merceena's. If the other names fail us we'll come back to her. The second apprentice was only a girl of twelve, so she was either turned out on her own or taken on by one of the older apprentices. The third was nearly sent away by Merceena several times for her stupidity and slovenly research habits, so it's not likely that she survived long enough to have become a wizard on her own. That means that the fourth name is the most likely suspect to have carried on Merceena's work."

"But the trail we need may not be any of these people Gran," Jamus stated. "It could have been an apprentice that gained her journeyman status and left long before Merceena died, or the person we need is the apprentice of the granddaughter of an apprentice."

"I will follow each in turn," shrugged Gran. "This isn't something I'm going into lightly, Jamus. But it is something that has to be done. You don't have to help."

Biting his lip the noble remained silent. Taking this as a sign of his acceptance Gran picked up her previous thoughts. "The fourth apprentice from the time of Merceena's death was named Ananeeda, and she was a relative of Merceena's, a great niece I believe, so she's the most likely choice."

Jamus tentatively held up a hand. "I think I know that name; wasn't she was the grandmother or something of the current Duke of Firth?"

Her eyes widening in sudden understanding, Gran pointed a finger at the viscount.

"By thunder, boy, you may have hit on it! The Weres and the

invasion of Aldrigal by Firth are connected, we all know that. It just makes sense! Ananeeda took Merceena's research notes with her and married the Duke of Firth, and continued her Were research! So long as she kept it undercover it would explain a great deal about what's going on now and during the last Were War!"

"So we're going to Firth?" demanded Tomo. "Despite the war?"

"No we aren't," replied Jamus happily. "At least, not right now; because we don't have to. Ananeeda eventually married the Duke of Firth but first she established a base of her own and willed it to the Signalers when she died. It's not that far away, it's not in Firth I mean, but it is across the mountains from here."

"Across the mountains?" moaned Tomo. "We can't cross them this late in the year; and the nearest pass is hundreds of miles away even if we could."

Gran cackled, slapping her knee so hard that three of her precious journals slid to the floor. Still laughing he scolded the men for their 'lack of faith'.

"So long as you're with me we'll find a way, like as not. My boy Mute knows the way, don't you?" she asked, jabbing a finger into her son.

Mute just looked confused and, for a long comical moment, sat with his mouth open and a distant look in his eyes. Then, like an ember being blown into full flame, the dawn of understanding appeared. Smiling back at Gran, though his was one of sick resignation rather than true mirth, he nodded slightly. Looking towards the other men he continued to nod; telling them that there was, indeed, a way to cross the mountains.

"I don't like that look, Mute," groaned Tomo.

"I have no idea what they're talking about and I'm getting sick over it already," agreed Jamus. "At least let me buy us some decent horses, and a carriage to travel in. That way no one will know who is inside."

"That didn't confuse that Were, now did it?" cackled Gran. "And where we're going there's likely to be more of those!"

By dawn the group had gathered up their belongings and packed them onto the new packhorse. The morning was frigid and the breath of each man froze in his facial hair before they were even out of site of the ruined building. Each had a pair of snowshoes but the going was so difficult that Mute considered making Gran ride the horse but the poor animal was already foundering in the drifts; forcing him to reject the idea. Making her accept a ride on his own back was just as difficult but not even her legendary switch could make him put her down once he had heaved her into place. Progress was slow but steady and by nightfall they had moved a little closer to the towering Kenebruks.

Camp that night was difficult; the snow was too dry to pack well so a shelter made of it was impractical and digging it away to build a fire meant shoveling out an incredible amount of snow. Once they did have a place cleared finding dry wood was an onerous chore. Gathering into Jamus' new, small tent with the fire before them, however, made all the work worthwhile.

"Where did Mute go?" asked Jamus, shivering noticeably as the fire's heat brought life back to his body.

"Out to scout," answered Tomo, his lips quivering.

"Doesn't he feel the cold?"

"Sometimes I don't think he does, not like we do anyway."

Neither man could remember a night colder than this one and since Gran wasn't saying much they suffered in their misery for a while, until finally the fire began to perk them back up. A rabbit Mute had plucked from its slumber roasted on a spit and Gran had dug enough of the tiny travel loaves from their pack to make a decent meal and the tantalizing aroma was making the bellies of all three growl loudly. Despite their hunger, relief from the cold was their first priority and they happily sat and soaked up the warmth.

Tomo reached for the meat only to have his hand slapped away by Gran.

"It's not done, you know it's not, now leave be," she said.

The soft thump of a powdery snowball struck the tent, the individual clumps of snow skittering down its canvas side. Glancing one to another Gran mouthed the word 'Mute' before sitting forward to peer from the tent. The horse, tied just behind the fire, stamped a hoof fitfully and then suddenly tried to rear as it neighed in terror. Forgetting their dinner and the fire's warmth the two men scrambled to string their bows as they tumbled from the tent, stepping around the fire and peering in the direction the snowball had come from just as another struck it.

It was dark but slivers of both moons were in the sky, their meager light reflecting off the snow to give them the ability to see a surprising distance. A figure was moving towards them, running if one can be said to run in deep snow while wearing snowshoes, and each raised their bow towards this figure before they realized that it was Mute. His eyes were wide, visible at such short distance, as the big man ran towards the camp. Behind him came a four-legged creature; a massive wolf who ran atop the snow as if on solid ground and was catching up to Mute as if he were standing still. Powerful and closing fast, no one who saw the beast could mistake it for a natural beast.

"Gran, it's a Were," Tomo cried, dropping the arrow he held and working desperately to open a long pouch in the back of his quiver. Jamus threw aside his bow completely and with a trembling hand drew a dagger from his belt; the edge of the blade shining oddly in the moonlight. Mute continued to run towards them; the wolf some distance behind but closing rapidly; it was unclear whether the woodsman would reach the camp before the beast caught him. Gran burst from the tent in a shower of snow, her silver coated frying pan gripped tightly in both hands.

Fear flooded them all and Gran's grin looked like that of a skull as she lifted her makeshift weapon and Tomo pulled forth the three silver-tipped arrows Jamus had bought for him in Skallist. In step they moved towards Mute in a grim line; knowing that their weapons were capable of damaging the Were but also aware that some of them would likely die in this fight.

"Here doggy, doggy," Gran whispered under her breath, her eyes shining with tears.

Tomo almost felt a flash of confidence at the old woman's anticipation, but it died immediately in the next instant.

That's when the second Were howled behind them.

# Chapter Thirty-Two

Mute lost a snowshoe as he reached the outer edge of the firelight, the sturdy construction of green branches and leather thongs flying off behind him as he struggled to escape the pursuing wolf-shaped monster. Spinning about he faced the charging Were for a moment, trying to set himself for the attack. As he planted his feet the unprotected boot broke through the snow and the big woodsman lost his balance, and then desperately threw himself onto his back to avoid his attacker. In mid-leap the beast tried to change direction, reaching down between its forepaws to snap at Mute's descending head as it passed, neatly biting off a stray lock of hair.

Breaking through the snow's crust as it landed, the beast was turning about to reach its prey even before its momentum was finished. Unable to defend himself, Mute lifted up his massive bow to meet the downward strike of the Were's jaws, catching the thick wood in the very back of the creature's mouth; doing no damage but deflecting the attack. Closing its teeth about the weapon, the Were tore it from Mute's hands and flicked it away with a snarl.

With a howl of mixed anger and fear, Gran charged the Were, crazed with the thought of the creature taking Mute from her in the same way that she had all but lost Albrim. Holding her silvered frying pan in both hands she brought the makeshift weapon back as far as she could and used all the strength in her body combined with her momentum to launch an attack at the Were. Screaming a wordless cry of fear she made contact with the creature's Cursed backside, driving a solid blow to its hip with a sharp crack of impact though it cost her balance. Yelping at the sting of the silver on his fur Burstis kicked back and then turned to finish the old woman where she now thrashed about in the snow. His rational mind considered the man he had been chasing as the greater threat; it had been the woodsman with his oversized bow that Burstis remembered from his attack on the carriage. Ignoring Gran where she lay face-down in the drift was difficult, but the Were pulled his gaze away to finish his first kill when a swift moving form coming from beyond the woman caught his eye.

When the growl of the second beast alerted them Tomo and Jamus instinctively spun about to face this newest threat. Tomo had a silvered arrow out and tried to load the bow and draw the string as he turned, hoping in the single instant that he had to find a simple wolf, or even one of the larger breed, but the sound of the beast had told the story; he knew what he was going to find. Lifting the bow he desperately tried to put the missile to the string as the half-man, half-wolf Were leaped at him. In the split instant he had to process the information he knew that he was going to be too late.

Jamus held his knife low, the blade carried a minor enchantment he hoped might penetrate a Were's magically enhanced hide. If he had had full access to his fortune he could have done better but under the circumstances it had been the best he had able to purchase in Skallist. Just a little slower reacting to the Were's growl, he had the advantage of not needing to load his weapon, so as the Cursed beast leaped at Tomo's throat the viscount instinctively brought the weapon up, catching the Were on its flank. Amazingly the Were twisted about in mid-air even as the blade struck, the monster's teeth missing their mark and causing its chest to strike Tomo in the face. As the man fell the Were threw out its hands to catch itself, forgetting once again in its rage that it only had one.

Albrim's snout dug into the snow, burying his head briefly before his good arm caught purchase on a hidden stone and he regained his balance. Bursting from the snow in a cloud of white the Were's eyes took in the various prey and his instincts locked onto the most dangerous predator in sight; the only one he felt could harm him despite the light line of pain from the knife wound on his hip. Albrim's mind reacted to the sudden appearance of his fellow Were and immediately went into the cycle of fight or flight. The scent of the other Were settled the matter, long had Albrim pursued him, and the one-armed Were used his momentum to leap again, passing over the prostrate Gran and slamming into Burstis.

One by one the humans struggled from the snow and took refuge across the fire from the snarling, battling Weres. They clutched their weapons as they watched the fight, each beast tearing at the other as they rolled about in snow that soon turned red from their blood. Albrim had the initial edge as he was in the larger half-wolf form while Burstis was in the faster four-legged shape of a full, though massive, animal. Seeing his disadvantage the more cunning and experienced Were used the fight's first lull to shift into the same form as his enemy, and then the advantage swung to Burstis with his two good arms.

The two Weres snarled and struggled, falling down only to stand up and rolling about madly as they fought. Crashing through the tent at one point Albrim found an opportunity when Burstis' head was briefly trapped beneath the canvass, and used the instant it took for the larger Were to escape to bite him deeply across the arm. Using his back legs much like a cat, Burstis clawed hard at Albrim's midsection, seeking to disembowel him as he twisted away. Clawing and biting the two beasts rolled through the fire several times, scattering the embers and ignoring any pain they might have felt from the flames as the smell of smoldering fur filled the campsite. Though both Weres were torn and bloody, those who watched the struggle knew that Albrim was taking the worst of it; the tainted blood staining the snow was mostly his.

"Shoot him!" Gran shrieked, pummeling Tomo with one hand as she searched for her dropped frying pan in the snow.

"Which one?" Tomo demanded, taking aim at the squirming, rolling bundle of fur.

"Not Albrim, you fool, the other one," Gran screeched, finding and jerking her frying pan free.

"He'll kill us the same as the other one," Jamus stated weakly, glad that Tomo was between he and Gran. He didn't want to be hit by the frying pan.

Moving the point of his silver arrow around, Tomo tried to comply but couldn't get a clear shot at Burstis without endangering Albrim. Briefly he considered just firing blindly into the pile, confident he would hit one of the Weres, but held off because of Gran's insistence. That one of these snarling beasts was the boy he had known was difficult for Tomo's practical side to accept, but he did not routinely disobey Gran.

With the light from the fire reduced, the battling Weres became seldom seen figures moving in and out of the shadows of the surrounding trees as well as in and out of the drifts enhanced by their earlier excavation. The moons still lit the landscape, but beneath the mostly evergreens visibility was practically nothing. Just as the two rolled behind a particularly large pine, a sharp bark of canine pain pierced the night air and more quickly than any of the humans could react, a lone Were darted around the tree and leaped among them.

Only Jamus and Mute acted before Burstis arrived, though the viscount's surprised stumble only accidentally brought his silvered knife up but in no way harmed the leaping Were, who batted the weapon away in mid-air. Mute managed a single step to place himself between the Were and Gran, and Burstis chose as his target the unarmed Mute whose bow lay broken in the snow. The two went down in a tangle, the Were intent on the human's throat and Mute trying to use the beast's momentum to flip it over him. Spinning with the two Tomo tried to get off a shot, but found himself in the same situation as before; unable to fire for fear of striking the wrong combatant. Gran swung her pan wildly, hitting nothing but air a long instant after the Were was past. Shrieking she chased after them, further blocking Tomo.

Burstis and Mute rolled over twice, the Were in charge of the roll as he was moving as soon as their momentum ceased. The big woodsman had been badly mauled in the short time, and lay unmoving as the Were moved on to his next victim. Leaping Burstis then charged at Jamus; the silver knife in his hand had not gone unnoticed. His face white with fear the nobleman held the blade out in front of him, all he had time to do before the Were reached him, and hoped that the creature would impale itself upon it.

Burstis was beginning to enjoy the fight now, and snarled in bestial glee as he contemplated killing each of these pitiful humans in turn. For the Were time had slowed to a crawl; even as his muscles bunched and then stretched with his leap, the movements of his enemies looked pitifully slow. The silver knife was there, but it was too low and Burstis knew he had timed his leap perfectly to pass over it. The old woman was too far away to do anything with her pitiful weapon and the big woodsman and the one-armed Were were already down. After all his weeks of pursuit he was looking forward to killing them all. He didn't even plan on taking his time with them; they'd die and he would revel in their slaughter, and feed like he had not had time to do in days. He'd forgotten Tomo, but remembered immediately when the arrow punched into his side.

Howling in pain unlike anything he'd experienced since he himself had gained the Curse, Burstis' hands caught the shoulders of the nobleman and drove the man into the snow. Using the man as a springboard Burstis changed directions, leaping at the bowman even as more of his blood pumped out of his wound and onto the snow, desperate to prevent the man from firing again. He misjudged the pain in his side, however, and fell well short of his target, sinking deep into the snow before encountering anything solid, and sprang again just as Tomo was placing his last silver arrow to the string. Even to Burstis, who viewed everything in the slow motion that fear and anger can bring, the man was lifting the bow impossibly fast. In that dreadfully detailed instant Burstis saw the arrow launched point blank into his chest, anticipating the sweet softness of the man's throat between his jaws. In such pain already he barely recognized the twin points of agony that exploded in his chest. Burstis snapped his jaws closed before the arrowhead pierced his Cursed heart.

Gasping and choking on his own blood Burstis collapsed atop Tomo, the Were still breathing but in agony so fierce he thought of nothing but gaining his next breath, his carnivore's instinct driving him to tear at the feeble man beneath him in his dying agony. That was not something Gran was going to allow. Hefting her frying pan, she stalked towards the Were.

# Epilogue

Gran tossed her bloody frying pan away as the Were ceased its final twitch; nothing remained of the creature's head save for a mishmash of blood and shattered bone and Gran herself was spattered with blood and brains over the front of her clothing. Slogging through the crimson-stained snow she moved to where she could see around the tree that concealed her grandson, moving over and kneeling down in the snow beside the broken, naked body of Albrim. He had shifted back to human form now, probably for the first time since the battle at the carriage. Gently she cradled him into her arms, then held his bloody face in her hands as she sobbed softly into the otherwise silent night. He was utterly limp, with no signs of life that she could see. His body was mangled; with long strips of flesh hanging away and blood splattered all over him. His face was relaxed, almost as if in a pleasant slumber, and his eyes were closed. He made no response as Gran settled him gently onto her lap.

"No, Albrim. Oh no."

# About the Author

Trevis Powell was born in rural Howevalley Kentucky and resides there with his wife and four children. After spending his school-age years more interested in sports than grades, he followed a six-year stint in the U.S. Army Reserves with various manual-labor intensive jobs. Eventually he went back to college, earning a degree in electronics.

After his marriage he settled down in his hometown and his creative desire, something he had dealt with since he was a teenager, finally became too strong to ignore and he began to write. Reading, and later gaming, had become outlets for his creative side and he noticed that his adventure designs and gaming worlds were always far more detailed than necessary to play a simple game.

Over time these became even more elaborate, and he finally had to admit that he needed more. Falling back on his natural story-telling ability he began to experiment with writing.

Two years later Trevis found his first publisher in Elmore Productions. Over the next five years he saw his name in print in a variety of outlets, including short stories, magazines, and gaming material. Again he found that he wanted more; feeling the need to develop the stories and characters he invented in greater detail. Now focusing on novels, Trevis is proud to be among the first authors in the new BlackWyrm Fiction line.

Also from BlackWyrm...

# Albrim's Curse

by Trevis Powell

All young Albrim wanted to be was a master bowman like his father. Then a savage attack on his home cost him his family, his arm, and his humanity – all at once! Crippled and contaminated by the Curse, his beloved Gran leaves him in the care of Mute, a giant warrior dedicated to protect-ing humanity from the depre-dations of the Quarg. Albrim does what he can to assist his master and redeem himself. But can a werewolf ever really recapture his humanity? [Epic Werewolf Fantasy, ages 14+]

# Gran's Secret

by Trevis Powell

Her son is dead; her grandson Cursed. Gran has to send him into hiding to protect him, and to protect others from him. But there are those who hunt Weres to use for their own evil purposes, and they are backed by the resources of kingdoms.

When these hunters begin snooping around Gran's village, there's nothing a sweet old lady can do to protect her grandson from such people, is there?

Apparently, you don't know Gran. [Epic Werewolf Fantasy, ages 14+]

www.BlackWyrm.com

## The Legend of Gwerinatha
### Branwen's Garden

by Brad Parnell

Young Robert journeys to another world. There he comes of age amid a feuding government, grotesque monsters, an ancient ancestor ...and a couple of teenaged girls. With the help of a young wolf named Louie, Robert is introduced to the wonders and perils of a strange land called Gwerinatha. [Allegoric Celtic Fantasy, ages 12+]

## The Legend of Gwerinatha
### Chaos' Corner

by Brad Parnell

Following Robert's footsteps into the magical land of Gwerinatha, Cameron Gray thought he'd check out a strange new world for a few minutes and be back for lunch. Instead he spends many years there learning how to become a survivor, a hunter, a warrior, and an unwitting catalyst for an alien's genocidal plot.
[Allegoric Celtic Fantasy, ages 12+]

www.BlackWyrm.com

by Jason Walters

At the edge of the known world, two desperate armies struggle for the right to siege a city that has never been taken. Terrible magics are unleashed and the fate of empires hangs in the balance. Highdome and his crew of cutthroats, monsters, and mutants don't care. They just want to stay alive. But when sorcery backfires and the fury of the Vast White desert is unleashed, the men and women of the Red Regiment must look inside of themselves to find the strength to survive.

[Dark Military Fantasy, ages 14+]

by Dirk Vandereyken

In a small village, a necromancer stands trial. At the center of the universe, the Spider that wove All watches intently. Webs are spun in the courtroom, of magic, of lies, and of scandal. The mage Baour argues that he supercedes not only man's laws, but god's! What he truly wants may only be uncovered through testimony. As strange magics meet strange deaths, can the reality behind it be unmasked? And should it?

[Fantasy Legal Thriller, ages 18+]

www.BlackWyrm.com

# SUGARLAND MELTING

by Sam Neace

An elderly millionaire named RJ Rockhouse opens a trailer park in eastern Kentucky, where he allows the tenants to live rent free, but the park isn't what it seems. Rockhouse is set to turn 100 years old, a sacred date for necromancers, which will allow him to transfer the spirits of himself and his wife into other bodies. Sugarland Melting is a passionate story of lost love, lost souls, betrayal, magic, and tragedy, with many surprises that will leave readers spellbound. [Urban Fantasy, ages 14+]

# The Veil

by Selina Fugate

A teenaged girl, Grace, draws the attention of an insane warlock. On the edge of death in a terrible accident, she makes a deal with Kracious, and is sucked into the warlock's sadistic game.

She meets a white witch that sets out to break her curse, but Kracious steps up the cat-and-mouse game with Grace's life to a new level.

Grace is suddenly shown the world behind "The Veil." A world with faeries, fallen angels, talking cats, and werewolves. A world she couldn't even imagine existed. [Teen Fantasy Horror, ages 12+]

www.BlackWyrm.com

# IMMORTAL BETRAYAL

by Paul Lewis

Darien, viking and explorer, braves the treacherous seas to discover new lands. That changes when he falls in love. But his world is shattered when he learns she has already been promised her to another. Darien's loyalty is put to the test as he battles vampires and werewolves. Darien finds himself having to choose between the woman he loves and his very soul. With tragic romance, heart stopping thrills, and plot twists, Immortal Betrayal aims to please.
[Tragic Fantasy Horror, ages 14+]

# IMMORTAL BURDEN

by Paul Lewis

**Immortal Burden** picks up where the first book in the immortal series, **Immortal Betrayal**, left off. It is now the 14th Century. To keep Darien from taking drastic measures he is summoned by Joshua, the first vampire, with a proposition. In exchange for his help Joshua will give him what he wants most. Darien is hesitant, but he would risk everything for a now distant dream.
[Tragic Fantasy Horror, ages 14+]